P9-DJK-466

"Do you want to play a game of b-ball?"

He picked up the basketball. His muscles flexed, causing her mouth to practically drop open. Jarred was all man. A handsome man full of sex appeal. After all these years, he still had an effect on her hormones. Nevealise couldn't deal with being up close and personal with him in a game of one-on-one. Not with the way her body was reacting to his mere presence. Instead of agreeing to the game, she took the cowardly way out.

"Maybe. I'd like to see the rest of the house first. If you don't mind."

"Sure. Come on." He threw the ball down, took her hand and led her back up the stairs.

With her senses already heightened, the warmth of his hand against hers had her tingling all over. So much so that she couldn't keep from shivering a bit. Her body's reaction to his was foreign. Sure, Nevealise had crushed on him for a long time, but this…this need was so strong it scared her.

Oh man, oh man, she chanted over and over in her head. *I am so in trouble.*

SHERWOOD FOREST LIBRARY
7117 W. SEVEN MILE RD.
DETROIT, MI 48221

JAN ' 2018
SF

Dear Reader,

My love for reading and writing romance has contributed greatly to my characters. I love what I do! Thankfully, I have been blessed tremendously by God to write about different family dynamics. Without my heavenly Father, I know I would not be able to do what I love—writing.

I would like to introduce to you the Manning dynasty. I have heard often enough, and it is my belief, that opposites do attract. Meet the first of the Manning brothers, Jarred Manning, and his feisty heroine, Nevealise Coleman. The suave take-no-prisoners hero Jarred has met his match in Nevealise, whom he has often referred to as "nerd girl." Oh, but wait! To Jarred's surprise, there's more to Nevealise than binary bytes. Much more.

I hope you enjoy Jarred and Nevealise's story just as much as I enjoyed writing it. I love hearing from readers. Drop me a line or two anytime :).

Cheers!

Serenity King

authorserenityking@gmail.com

SerenityKing.com

SerenityKingExpressions.Blogspot.com

Facebook.com/Serenity.King

Twitter.com/SerenitysCircle

Love me FOREVER

SERENITY KING

HARLEQUIN® KIMANI™ ROMANCE

If you purchased this book without a cover you should be aware that this book is stolen property. It was reported as "unsold and destroyed" to the publisher, and neither the author nor the publisher has received any payment for this "stripped book."

Recycling programs for this product may not exist in your area.

ISBN-13: 978-0-373-86496-6

Love Me Forever

Copyright © 2017 by Letricia Gortman

All rights reserved. The reproduction, transmission or utilization of this work in whole or in part in any form by any electronic, mechanical or other means, now known or hereinafter invented, including xerography, photocopying and recording, or in any information storage or retrieval system, is forbidden without written permission. For permission please contact Harlequin Kimani, 225 Duncan Mill Road, Toronto, Ontario M3B 3K9, Canada.

This is a work of fiction. Names, characters, places and incidents are either the product of the author's imagination or are used fictitiously, and any resemblance to actual persons, living or dead, business establishments, events or locales is entirely coincidental.

® and TM are trademarks of Harlequin Enterprises Limited or its corporate affiliates. Trademarks indicated with ® are registered in the United States Patent and Trademark Office, the Canadian Intellectual Property Office and in other countries.

For questions and comments about the quality of this book please contact us at CustomerService@Harlequin.com.

HARLEQUIN®
www.Harlequin.com

Printed in U.S.A.

Serenity King is a *USA TODAY* bestselling author. She has been reading romances since she was sixteen years old and her auntie first placed a Harlequin book in her hands. Now King writes contemporary and erotic romances that feature men's fierce devotion to resilient women. She has a strong passion for family-oriented alpha men who live, love and fight for their women. She has been a published author since 2010 and has more than eighteen titles under her belt.

Serenity currently lives in the New York area with her husband and children. King loves feedback and welcomes readers to email her at authorserenityking@gmail.com. Visit her at website at serenityking.com or her blog at serenitykingexpressions.blogspot.com.

Books by Serenity King

Harlequin Kimani Romance

Love Me Forever

To my wonderful husband and children,
thank you for all of your encouragement.
I could not continue to do what I do without your love
and support. When I wanted to throw in the towel,
you all stood behind me, pushing me forward and
compelling me to follow my dream. You all rock!
I love you from the bottom of my heart.

My bestie, Dora, your prayers, support and friendship
have always meant so much to me. Outside of my
family, you are my rock of reason as well as my
inspiration to work hard and to always put God first.
Love you to the moon and back.

My awesome parents and siblings, you all know you
rock so hard. Each one of you and your individual
creativity has always been an inspiration to me.
You guys keep me laughing and just enjoying life.
You all know you're crazy, right? *snicker*

Yvette Hines, Yvonne Nicholas, Jayha Leigh
and Jeanie Johnson, you all are just too good to me.
Big hugs and much love.

Acknowledgments

To my fans. This series is for you.
Thank you for your patience and your support.
Remember when choosing a mate…choose wisely.
Enjoy the romance!

Smooches <3

To God be all the glory!

Chapter 1

"What in the world have you gotten us into, Dad?" Jarred muttered, a frustrated sigh escaping his lips. He'd been scrutinizing legal documents for what felt like hours and still didn't have any answers to his many questions about one of their newer acquisitions, Tempest Mortgage.

Jarred Manning had always thought he had it all: a comfortable, enviable career as lead attorney for Manning Enterprises, a multimillion-dollar banking corporation, wealth and a beautiful brownstone in the Park Slope neighborhood of Brooklyn, New York. Until the Tempest Mortgage deal.

Just before his scheduled retirement, Jarred's father, William Manning, the founder of the family corporation, had purchased Tempest, a failing mortgage company, from his close friend Josiah Tempest—and promptly turned Jarred's comfortable life into a constant treadmill of work. Instead of spending his nights in the arms of a beautiful woman, he now spent them at his Manhattan office.

William Manning had started the company slowly. An investment banker, he'd purchased one bank and then another. When Jarred and his two brothers had come into the company they'd added two more banks, just within the last five years, and as recently as a year ago the corporation had acquired a small chain of banks that specialized in mortgages for low-income families. All sound business decisions. But Jarred could not understand the last takeover his father had spearheaded, a few months ago—the in-the-red Tempest Mortgage Company.

Nor could he understand how his father had promptly retired as CEO of Manning Enterprises right after that and moved with their mom back to his birthplace of Paris, Texas, where they owned a farmhouse. William had handed the reins of Manning Enterprises to Jarred and his younger brothers, Langston and Brice. An attorney himself, Langston often worked closely with Jarred, while Brice, the financial wiz of the family, preferred to operate on the business services side.

Only their sister, Katherine, the youngest of the four siblings, didn't enter the family business. Though she held a degree in political science, the free-spirited Kat was pursuing a degree in interior design at FIT, the Fashion Institute of Technology.

Once again Jarred scanned the numbers and sighed. "I'm convinced that I'm being punished for something," he groaned. Yes, that had to be it. Why else would he be stuck in the office well past business hours, working on this nightmare of a venture called Tempest? He grumbled, frustrated with everything about his new duties.

There were a rapid three knocks on Jarred's office door before it pushed open and his brother, Langston, walked in. *What now?* Jarred took a deep breath, sat up in his chair and ran his hand across his bearded face. He could tell from the stiff way that Langston moved, his appearance harried, not to mention the ferocious scowl on his face, that something or someone had him pissed.

At six feet, Langston was an inch shorter than Jarred, and he was two years younger than his own thirty-four years of age. They shared the same strong jawline and thick brows that accentuated hazel eyes, but Langston kept his wavy hair close-cropped to his head, and sported little more than a five o'clock shadow, with a mustache he kept neatly trimmed.

Jarred watched as his brother stormed across the plush carpet to one of the leather wingback chairs, then plopped down with a heavy sigh.

"What's wrong now?" Jarred asked, eyeing him closely. Langston was a rather easygoing guy, but it looked as if he hadn't slept in a few days.

"The question should be what is not wrong?" he responded sourly. "This acquisition is going to be the death of us all. Maybe we should have listened to Brice on this one. This is a huge headache times three."

Jarred knew exactly what headache his brother was referring to. Tempest.

Josiah Tempest was a longtime friend of their father's and had taught William Manning most of what he knew about the banking industry. Unfortunately, years later, Josiah's failing health and poor management decisions had caught up with him, which now left the Manning brothers with a mess to clean up.

"Where's Brice?" Jarred asked, his voice sounding as tired as he was.

"I haven't a clue. Probably between the thighs of a beautiful woman, which is where we all should be, instead of in the office at nine o'clock on a Friday evening."

Jarred groaned, pushed back in his chair, linked his fingers behind his head, closed his eyes and let out a frustrated breath. "In the arms of a beautiful woman seems to be a thing of the past. At least until we get some semblance of control over the situation with Tempest," he said, opening his eyes and looking at his brother.

"I can see why Tempest's sons decided to become doctors. Their father is great at giving business advice and helping others, but he sure as hell didn't apply any of that knowledge to his own corporate dealings."

"You're right about that. To be fair, everything was running well for a long while. I can't point my finger to exactly where it all began to unravel, other than when he took ill. But I still say something else had to have been happening on the inside. We need Brice to bring us up to speed on the most recent financials. The ones I'm looking at now are horrid." Jarred ran his hands across his face once more. Work had always given him a sense of fulfillment, but now he just felt burdened by it all. He needed something different. What, he wasn't sure. And he had no time to figure it out.

Langston's reply caught his attention. "Well, good luck with that. Brice told Dad from the very start not to take over this business. Not only did Dad not listen to him, but he went off and retired to some faraway place." He threw up his hands in frustration.

"Please, don't get me started on that." Jarred snorted. "Dad hadn't lived in his hometown since he was a kid, and then *boom*, he suddenly got a 'hankering' to return." He shook his head and rested it against his chair again.

Jarred could feel Langston eyeing him. "You're unusually quiet. What's wrong?"

He pinned his brother with a look. "How am I quiet if I'm talking to you?"

"You know what I mean. No ranting?"

He shrugged. "I've been venting all week. Trust me, it hasn't been pretty. Shelley has suddenly decided to take a leave of absence," Jarred grunted. Shelley, his assistant, had been working for him for only a short time, but had worked for Manning Enterprises for a few years.

Langston chuckled. "That bad, huh?"

"Apparently."

"You're not exactly known for your decorum, Jarred. I'm surprised she hasn't left sooner. I hope you know she's probably looking for another position." Langston chuckled again.

"Brice slept with her. I'm sure of it. Shelley's pissed because according to her, 'He's ignoring me,'" Jarred mimicked, and then scowled. He haphazardly moved things around on his desk. Still annoyed, he tossed a single piece of paper across the top. It landed on the floor, which sent Langston into a fit of laughter.

"Now that's more like the Jarred I know."

"What am I supposed to do, Langston? I'm his

brother, not his damn keeper. Although at the rate he's going, he clearly needs a caretaker or something."

Brice was a serial dater. His nonchalant ways with women were surely going to come back to haunt him one day. Jarred didn't think his baby brother had ever been in a serious relationship, though there was that one time after college when Brice had been unusually snarly and impossible to live with. Jarred assumed a woman was the reason. At their parents' twenty-fifth wedding anniversary, Brice had brought one woman to the party, left and come back with another. That little stint hadn't gone over well with their mother. Delores "Dee" Manning had read Brice the riot act. Brice had looked contrite and vowed never to disrespect the family like that again. His brother still dated a lot of women, he just never brought them around the family, and, as he put it, never to his place.

Langston leaned back in his chair. "Brice swears he's never slept with Shelley. Only took her out a few times. She wanted a relationship, and according to our brother, that was out of the question. I keep telling him that if he continues to play with women like this, it's going to come back and bite him on the ass." Langston took a deep breath. "We both need a break from here for a little while. You're just so wrapped up in this business you can't see the forest for the trees. All of it will be here on Monday, ready and waiting for us. Let's go somewhere where there's good food, live entertainment and relaxation."

"And where would that be?" Jarred furrowed his brow, and a huge smile covered Langston's face.

"What?" Jarred questioned.

"I know this great spot. It's in Jersey and it's perfect! Each night there's something different going on—from spoken word, to live bands, to solo artists, you name it. A classy place, too. A relaxing atmosphere all around," Langston said.

"The last time you took me to a place that *supposedly* had a nice atmosphere, I was looking for someone to hand me some flowers and a pamphlet, and point me to a cabbage, claiming it to be the Chosen One," Jarred mocked, rolling his eyes and making a face.

"It was a retreat that focused on getting in touch with oneself. Everyone hugged. It was supposedly a way of being respectful and free." Langston chuckled. "Besides, I was in college, bro. Different values and ideals back then," he explained. "You're never going to let me forget it, are you?"

"No, never." Jarred glared at him. In retrospect, the place really wasn't that bad; he just liked to give his brother a hard time. Although back then he really did think Langston was into some kind of cult. No doubt thanks to that girl he was dating, who was, in Jarred's opinion, weird.

"Come on, Jarred, it will be good for you to get away from this office. When was the last time you went out and had fun? I know you don't like the club scene, but you need to get free from this place for a while. The only thing you do is work. As a matter of fact, when was the last time you went out on a date?"

"I've gone out on dates, Langston," he grumbled, lowering his head to avoid eye contact. The truth of the matter was ever since his ex-fiancée, Lainey, ran out on him and eloped with someone he thought was a close friend, Jarred hadn't any trust in the opposite sex. That was two years ago. The sting of betrayal still lingered.

Jarred and Lainey had dated on and off all through college. They'd parted when Lainey went abroad for her graduate studies and he had gone on to law school, but then reconnected upon her return to the States. To him it was as if they'd never separated. They got engaged and were planning a life together. He thought they had the same aspirations for their future. Evidently not, he found out, when Lainey left him with an empty house and a brief note. Apparently she was in love with their mutual friend Braxton—the man she eloped with.

"Snap out of it, Jarred," Langston said, no doubt seeing him lapse into a trip down memory lane. "You get an itch, you scratch it and then move on. Since Lainey left, you've never gone out with the same woman twice. Anyway, this is not about dating—it's about you not running yourself into the ground with work. Take a break," he pleaded. "I promise this place is great, and you'll have a good time."

"How did you find it?"

"Brice," Langston murmured, and lowered his head.

"Hell, no!" Jarred said emphatically. "I know you didn't just try to convince me to go somewhere based on our brother's recommendation."

"It's not his recommendation. I've been there and it's cool. Trust me."

Jarred sighed heavily. He really didn't feel like being bothered tonight. He would've preferred a hot meal, some relaxing jazz music and maybe catching a basketball game on television.

"If this is one of those touchy-feely places, I'm going to kick your ass," Jarred said.

"You and what army are going to kick my ass?" Langston sniffed.

"The army of left and right," Jarred said, balling his hands into fists and lifting them one at a time.

"Whatever. Lock up. I'll meet you at the elevators downstairs. I need to collect my briefcase and jacket." Langston stood and walked to the door.

"I'm going to give Brice a call before I leave, so give me about ten to fifteen minutes." Jarred settled back in his chair.

"Doubt if you'll be able to reach him, but will do." Langston stepped out of the office.

Jarred watched the door close behind him and then took out his cell phone and dialed Brice's number. The phone rang three times before his brother answered, with a barked, "Hello."

"What the hell is wrong with you?" Jarred asked, irritated. "You were supposed to be in the office."

"Who says I wasn't? What do you want?" Brice huffed. It seemed as if he didn't want to be bothered.

"If you can snatch yourself away from whatever or whoever it is that has you over the top, Langston and I are going to some spot that you took him to in Jersey."

"Heavens?"

"Heavens what?" Jarred asked.

"That's the name of the lounge—Heavens. What time are you leaving?"

"We're out of here in about fifteen minutes."

Before Jarred could say another word, Brice tersely said goodbye and hung up.

I'm going to choke the daylights out of him one day, Jarred thought as he gathered up his belongings. He made sure to also collect the Tempest documents. He had endless hours of work ahead of him, but Langston was right. It was a Friday night, and Jarred was long overdue to let loose. Sure, he had the occasional romp, so to speak, but most of his dating for the past two years was to appease his bruised ego over his failed relationship. It had been a while since he'd just hung out and enjoyed a night out with the guys. He wasn't in favor of the bar scene much anymore. He'd been there, done that in college. Now he needed a place to just sit back and relax and not worry about expectations from anyone.

Jarred locked the office, then took the elevator down to the ground floor, where Langston was waiting.

"Are we taking your car or mine?" his brother asked.

Jarred shrugged. "It doesn't matter to me."

"Well, look who has decided to join us." Langston smiled.

Jarred glanced over his shoulder and saw Brice coming through the door of the stairwell, appearing out of sorts. The jacket of his dark Armani suit and his tie were hanging over his shoulder. He looked like he'd sounded on the phone: miserable. Brice had inherited their mother's silver-gray eyes, and his complexion was a shade darker than Jarred and Langston's honey-wheat skin tones. His rumpled appearance only confirmed to Jarred that all three of them were at their wits' end.

"I'm taking my own ride. I may leave with company, so I'll meet you two there," Brice said as he walked past them.

"Where are you coming from?" Jarred arched a brow at his baby brother. Brice had led him to believe that he'd been in the office, but not that he was still present.

"IT department. I told you I was here," Brice replied.

"What were you doing in IT?" Langston asked.

Brice stopped, turned around and glared at them. "Working. Now, are we going to Heavens or not?"

"Yes, but what has you in such a foul mood?" Langston inquired.

"I'm not in a foul mood. I'm in a bad mood, plain and simple. So, are we going or am I to find my entertainment elsewhere?"

"By all means, bro, let's ride." Langston gestured toward their parked vehicles.

"I'm just warning you two. The minute somebody hands me one of those 'get in touch with your inner self' pamphlets, I am kicking both of your asses," Jarred interjected, pointing at his brothers.

"You might whip Langston, but you ain't beating me," Brice snorted.

Jarred playfully punched his shoulder. "You may be taller than me and Langston, but I can still drop you, baby bro. Don't let me school you out here in these streets."

"Man, listen to you trying to act hard. Dude, we grew up in the suburbs," Brice retorted, and sent them all into a fit of laughter.

"How far away is this place?" Jarred rounded the car to the passenger door.

"About forty-five minutes to an hour, depending on traffic," Langston said.

Jarred climbed into the passenger seat, put his briefcase on the floor in front of him and sighed deeply. He loved his brothers, but they drove him crazy.

The smooth sound of Kenny G was playing through the surround sound. *Yes.* Jarred rested his head back and relaxed to the flawless notes the saxophone belted out.

Chapter 2

They pulled into the packed parking lot of a one-story building surrounded by dark, tempered-glass windows. A hand-painted sign that hung above the door read Heavens, with musical symbols on each side. A line snaked out the door and down the walkway on three sides of the building.

"It's crowded tonight," Langston said.

"Appears that way," Jarred responded.

"I'm going to follow Brice. He knows this place inside and out. He'll know where there's parking."

"I thought you'd been here before?"

"I have. It's just been a while."

They found parking a block away from the lounge. Jarred was surprised that by the time they walked back around to the club, the crowd had practically disappeared.

"Where did all those people go?" he asked.

"Most probably weren't allowed inside, so they left. There is a dress code. No jeans or sneakers. Business casual is the preference," Brice said, as they walked up to the door.

The bouncer, a tall man with a large build and a buzz cut, stood there. "Brice, my man! I haven't seen you here in a little bit. Go on in. You know your table is always available."

"Thanks, Norman. How's it going?"

"I can't complain. The lady herself is here tonight. You all are in for a treat." Norman smiled.

"She's back?"

"Yep, and on fire. Go on in. She'll be on in a few."

"Thanks, man. I'll talk to you later. By the way, these are my brothers, Jarred and Langston. Langston's been here before with me, but you weren't on duty," Brice said.

"Nice to meet you. Go on inside." Norman waved Brice through. Jarred and Langston followed on his heels.

"Is there anyone he doesn't know?" Jarred whispered to Langston.

"Our brother does get around. I'm wondering who this *she* is."

"I can hear you two," Brice snorted.

"So?" Jarred and Langston responded simultaneously.

Brice led them to a table in front of a dimly lit stage. A gold Reserved sign sat on the table.

Jarred glanced around the lounge. The place seemed like one giant booth, with leather seating and lit candles in rust-colored holders giving the room an orange glow. Very cozy, he had to admit, very relaxing. This was a place one would want to come after a hard day. The round table that he and his brothers occupied could easily fit eight people.

"So who is this *she* the bouncer was referring to, Brice?" Langston asked.

"You'll see, Lang my boy." Brice smirked.

"If you call me Lang again, you won't be seeing anything or anybody," Langston countered.

Jarred chuckled. *Brotherly love. What can I say? Nothing, and that's what I'll do. Say nothing.*

A big, circular spotlight lit the center of the stage, and people began to stand and clap.

Jarred eyed all of them suspiciously. There was no one on the stage. A few moments later, a lone figure walked out into the center and Jarred's mouth dropped open. The woman had legs that went on for days. They were displayed in a formfitting black dress with a deeply cut V neckline and a long, almost waist-high split up the side. Her natural hair was styled in a thick, wavy bob that stopped at her shoulders. Her skin tone was slightly darker than caramel, but lighter than pecan, more like cinnamon. Her body was to die for, and her smile shone brighter than the stage lighting.

"If you don't close your mouth soon, bro, you are sure to attract flies," Brice said.

"You all sure know how to make a lady feel loved," the mystery lady said. Her voice was so sultry and soulful, a shiver of awareness coursed through Jarred.

He could do nothing but stare at her, spellbound by her presence. He squinted his eyes and leaned forward to get a better view. Upon closer inspection, he recognized that there was something familiar about her, then it hit him like a sack of bricks.

"Hey, isn't that—"

"Nerd Girl," Langston finished.

"Be quiet, you two. Her name is Nevealise not Nerd Girl," Brice said angrily.

"We know her name, Brice," Jarred countered. "It was just an expression and you know it. We all called her that back then."

The last time Jarred saw Nevealise, she was headed to Cambridge for her freshman year at MIT. Jarred had known from his sister that she had a crush on him. Nevealise had been Kat's friend and math tutor, and was often at the house. Kat had kidded him often enough about her friend's crush. However, he had no interest in the young woman who, at eighteen, was six years his junior. Jarred remembered he'd called her "Jailbait." At the time he considered her far too young for him. Besides, he was already in a relationship with Lainey.

Well, I'll be damned. Little Nevealise Tempest has grown into a stunning woman.

She used to come around with her father, and usually had a book in her hand. He and his brothers had dubbed her "Nerd Girl" because she was always spouting something she'd discovered in a book, and was a whiz at equations. Her visits with her father were what led her to become his sister's tutor. If he remembered correctly, she was two years older than Kat, which would put Nevealise at around twenty-eight now. No longer jailbait. If he was honest with himself he'd admit the moment their eyes met, he wanted to drag her offstage and have his way with her.

"What the hell is she doing, singing in a club? Didn't she graduate from MIT?" Jarred murmured.

"Damn, she is fine," Langston declared.

Just then Nevealise bellowed out a soulful rendition of Joss Stone's "Put Your Hands On Me."

That voice. It held Jarred captive. He couldn't turn away even if he tried. Not only was she beautiful, but her singing was glorious.

"Does her old man know that his daughter is a lounge singer?" Jarred asked.

"None of her family knows. For the record, she isn't only a singer, she owns the place. Hence the name," Brice told them.

"Who cares whether or not her family knows? She's good," Langston said, bopping to the tune.

Like magnet to metal, Jarred and Nevealise's eyes met and lingered. She was the first to break eye contact as she finished the song and transitioned directly into another. This time she sauntered out into the crowd, stopping at their table to place a kiss on Brice's cheek. She flashed Jarred and Langston a quick smile, then continued mingling with the other guests. For the first time in his life, Jarred was jealous of his youngest brother.

"Don't get your hackles up, big brother. Nev and I are just friends," Brice snorted.

"What are you going on about, Brice? What hackles?" Jarred said, unable to take his eyes off the woman.

Langston chuckled. "Who are you kidding? You practically came out of your seat when Nerd Girl kissed Brice's cheek. That scowl didn't help, either."

Jarred sent Langston a scathing look that could have melted iron. "What I don't understand is why are we killing ourselves with her father's mess and she's out here having the time of her life?" he retorted.

"You can't blame that on her. Her father never wanted her to have any dealings with the business, even after she graduated top of her class at MIT. She did what she had to do, and she does it well," Brice said proudly. "Besides, it's our mess now. We acquired the company, remember?"

Jarred didn't say anything further. He sat back and listened intently as she sang. He would have been content listening to her all night if he didn't have an erection that was making it impossible to be comfortable no matter what he did. He squirmed in his seat, trying to adjust his trousers, which were continually growing tighter.

He gazed at Nevealise just as she moved her head in their direction. His lips lifted in a slow smile, and then he winked at her, causing her to miss a beat. Not that anyone would notice. Oh, but he did. *Gotcha!* It appeared he still had some kind of effect on her. *My night has just taken a very interesting turn,* he thought, and he hoped to enjoy it to the fullest.

Chapter 3

Nevealise startled a bit as Jarred Manning winked at her. What was he playing at? Better yet, what was he doing here? Although she hadn't seen him in years, Nevealise didn't figure Heavens would be a hangout for the oldest Manning brother. Closing her eyes, arms stretched out in front of her, she let the smooth sounds of Ella Fitzgerald's "Cry Me a River" run flawlessly from her lips. After she finished her number, Nevealise opened her eyes to another standing ovation.

"Thank you, thank you." She smiled, looked around the packed lounge, bowed and then walked offstage, but not before she caught the eye of Jarred again. He was standing, smiling and clapping heartily along with the crowd. Taking a deep breath, she briskly exited and headed to her dressing room.

Nevealise flashed the bodyguard standing by her

door a quick smile, and proceeded inside. She plopped down on the chair in front of the vanity and mirror, and released a long breath she hadn't known she'd been holding. She placed her hand on her abdomen, trying to calm the butterflies having a party in her stomach. She stared at her reflection in the mirror. The hazel eyes that stared back at her showed how she felt: nervous.

"Oh, goodness," she chanted a few times, before picking up the bottle of chardonnay she always had waiting for her when she left the stage, and pouring a couple ounces into her tulip-shaped wineglass. She sipped a little bit at a time, wanting to savor the taste.

Seeing Jarred Manning again had stirred up feelings in her that Nevealise thought she'd long forgotten. Feelings she had long ago filed away as her first teenage crush. Tonight Jarred's bold stare had her insides quivering straight to her core, causing her to cross her legs, trying to stem the vibrations she felt there.

Nevealise had felt daring as she'd sauntered out into the crowd and stopped at their table. She'd kissed Brice on the cheek, only to look up and catch Jarred's molten gaze. Her eyes instantly zoomed in on his full, kissable lips. Her sassy move to show the brothers that she was no longer the girl they often referred to as "Nerd Girl," that she was in fact a woman in charge of her sexuality, had backfired on her.

Who was she kidding? At the mere presence of Jarred she'd become a nervous wreck, almost dropping in a dead faint to the floor. It should be a sin to be so fine. The handsome devil knew he'd gotten to her when he'd winked at her. Although she'd recovered quickly, she'd missed a beat in the number she was performing. Jarred had arrogantly smiled and lifted his glass to her.

Enough thinking about Jarred Manning. She needed to bring her body under control. Nevealise was reacting to him like she was a sexually charged teenager. Her mind knew that; however, her body moved to its own beat, and was having the hots for Jarred Manning.

Sighing deeply, Nevealise took another sip of her wine. "Ah, just what I need," she murmured, then leaned back in the chair, lifted her face to the ceiling and closed her eyes. The wine usually calmed her after a performance, and tonight she needed it more than ever. The sight of Jarred in the audience had frayed her nerves. What was he doing here? "Ugh!" she cried. "Get out of my head, Jarred!"

Nevealise jolted at the knock on her door. The sound vibrated like a thunderbolt in the peace and tranquility of her quiet dressing room. Her hand pressed against her chest, trying to stem her racing heart. Mentally shaking herself, Nevealise got up and looked at the closed door.

"Who's there?"

"It's me, Nev. Can I come in?"

Nevealise smiled at the briskness of Brice's voice. He always sounded as if he was angry or in a hurry. While attending college Nevealise had become friends with an engineering student, Jasmine Greene, who unbeknownst to her was dating Brice Manning. Lovers of the written word, Jasmine and Brice would often drag Nevealise along to lounges and clubs to listen, and sometimes participate, in song and the spoken word. It was during those times with Jasmine and Brice that she'd discovered her passion for singing.

Jasmine and Brice were the only two people out-side her immediate family who were aware of her dis-dain for her father, and their tumultuous relationship. To this day Jasmine was still Nevealise's best friend, and Brice had become more of a brother than a friend. He was the person who'd helped her make Heavens a reality, investing in her talent as well as her business.

"Nev, are you all right? Can I come in?"

He was alone. *What a relief.* She sat down, smiled and called out, "Sure. Come on in, Brice."

Nevealise watched as the door slowly opened a bit and Brice stuck his head in. That surprised her, be-cause he usually just walked in.

"What are you doing?" She frowned.

"Just making sure you're decent," he responded, be-fore pushing the door open and strolling in. Nevealise's stomach dropped as Langston and Jarred followed close behind, piling into her dressing room.

The knot in her stomach felt as if she'd swallowed a brick. *Ah, hell*, she thought, as she saw Jarred standing there staring at her with a smirk on his oh-so-handsome face. Nevealise never really cared for bearded men, but Jarred wore his well. His was light, neatly trimmed and seemed to complement his thick eyebrows, honey-brown skin tone and those hazel eyes that seemed to look straight to her soul. If she wouldn't appear child-ish, she would have rolled her eyes at the self-assured oldest Manning brother. Instead, she turned her mega-watt smile onto Brice.

"Brice," she said, standing to embrace him with a gentle hug. "You didn't tell me that the Brothers Three would be gracing me with your presence tonight."

"That's because I didn't know. Spur-of-the-moment

thing. On top of that, I didn't know you were in town. You didn't call," Brice said. "It's been too long, Nev."

Nevealise backed out of his embrace and looked him in the eye. "Like you—spur-of-the-moment thing."

"How long will you be in town?" Brice asked. After graduating from MIT, Nevealise had stayed on in the area, making Cambridge, Massachusetts, her home.

"Not sure." She looked over Brice's shoulder at Langston. He had been the more laid-back one, she remembered, and he'd always been nice to her. Compassionate and patient. She knew his referral to her as Nerd Girl was not malicious. In fact, most times he'd pulled her ponytail when he'd called her that. She hadn't seen Langston in years. Or Jarred, for that matter.

Brice must have noticed her eyes flittering about the room, because he said, "You remember my brothers, Langston and Jarred?"

"It's been a while, but of course I remember them," she said.

Langston held out his hand. "You have a beautiful voice. I really enjoyed the show."

Nevealise shook it. "Not the 'Nerd Girl' you remember," she teased.

Langston had the nerve to blush. "Yes, about that. We were young and full of ourselves," he said, clearing his throat.

"No worries. It never bothered me. I was and still am a nerd and proud of it. Well, not at the time." She chuckled.

Nevealise was surprised when Brice pulled her into the crook of his arm. She turned her face up and gave him a questioning look. He just winked at her. *What in the world is he playing at?*

"I'm Jarred," she heard his other brother say. The seductive timbre of Jarred's voice captivated her, compelling her to look at him. His hand was outstretched, so she had no choice but to extend hers. He grasped her hand as if it were a lifeline and glided his thumb over her knuckles.

"I didn't know you and Brice were an item," he said smoothly.

Nevealise was caught off guard by him having his way with her hand, and then by his assumption that she and Brice were a couple. She was stunned to silence until she felt the firm squeeze of Brice's palm on her shoulder.

"You still don't," she gathered herself enough to say. "Brice and I are friends. Not lovers. He's more like a brother." Nevealise didn't know why she felt compelled to explain their relationship. She didn't owe anyone an explanation, least of all Jarred Manning. "Can I have my hand back now?" she said, trying to pull it from his grasp. He refused to let go.

"If we were an item, I believe I would take exception to you holding my woman's hand as if you were waiting for an opportunity to bed her," Brice chided. "I believe the lady asked for it back."

"Uh, bro, you can't hold her hand hostage," Langston interjected with a chuckle.

Nevealise darted her gaze from one brother to the other, all the while trying to disengage her hand from Jarred's. Langston apparently thought it funny, but Jarred's eyes were not so happily fixed on Brice.

"We are not a couple," Brice stressed. Nevealise could hear the smugness in his voice. "I told you, Nev and I are friends."

The brothers had had a conversation about her? When? And more importantly, why?

"What's going on, Brice?"

"Nothing, Nev. Just my big brother being his normal presumptuous self. Are you performing all weekend?"

"I haven't decided yet. Playing it by ear at this point."

"Have you spoken to your father yet?"

Nevealise tensed. "No, and I hadn't planned on it," she said easily.

"Maybe you should," Jarred interposed.

Her father was a sore point with her, and she didn't appreciate Jarred trying to tell her what to do.

"As I said, I don't plan on speaking to him. And let go of my hand," she snapped, finally snatching it out of his grasp.

"Do you have real daddy issues, or are you just throwing a tantrum?" Jarred asked.

Nevealise's eyes flashed fire. "Excuse you! Throwing a tantrum! What am I, three? You don't know me, so I suggest you keep your comments to yourself, especially where my father and I are concerned." Nevealise breathed hard. The rapid rise and fall of her chest was a telltale sign that she was angry. No, she wasn't angry. She was furious. Her father was a touchy subject, and for this know-it-all to assume she was the problem had her enraged.

"Calm down, Nev. Jarred's just upset about the situation," Brice said.

"Jarred, she's right," Langston interjected. "You have no business making assumptions about her and her father. You owe Nevealise an apology."

"What situation?" Nevealise asked, perplexed. She

was trying her best to follow the conversation, but couldn't. What were they talking about? Apparently, whatever it was had something to do with her father. If so, she didn't much care. As long as she wasn't involved.

"What am I supposed to think when her father has left us with his mess of a company?" Jarred said.

"Wrong." Brice shook his head. "Dad had a choice and he made it."

"What mess? What's he talking about, Brice?" Nevealise huffed. Oh, how she hated secrets. Hated them with a passion.

"I'll explain later. This is not the time nor the place. Can you come by my house tomorrow? I'll explain everything," Brice stated.

"*We'll* explain," Jarred said.

Before anyone could say anything else, there was a loud knock on the door. "Nev, is everything okay in there?" Norman's booming voice sounded through the panel.

"Everything's fine, Norman," she said, rushing to the door and pulling it ajar. Norman pushed the door open farther to peek inside. He glanced over at Brice, nodded and closed the door, apparently satisfied that she was, indeed, fine. When she turned back to her guests, she noticed Jarred looked as if he was rearing up for another altercation with Brice. And he'd accused her of acting like a child? Go figure.

Nevealise crossed her arms and looked at Brice. "I have a full morning and I'll probably be back here tomorrow night. What time should I come?"

"Why don't we make it Sunday, so no one has to rush?" Jarred suggested, cutting in.

"Sunday's better for me, too," Langston said.

"Brunch on Sunday. How's that?" Brice asked her. "My place."

"Sunday brunch is okay with me." Nevealise shrugged. "Just know that if this has anything to do with me helping my father in any way, I'm not listening, nor will I help."

"We'll discuss this further on Sunday, Nev. That's the point of the brunch," Brice snickered.

"I'm just saying. You know my stance on my father, Brice."

"Yeah, yeah, yeah. You say it often enough. Are you going back on tonight?" he asked, changing the subject, for which she was grateful. She didn't feel like another showdown with Jarred.

"Maybe. Maybe not." She smiled. "In any event I need to change out of this gown. Getting kind of sticky," she said, wiggling her hips.

"I can take a hint. She's trying to get rid of us. Come on, you two, let's give Nev her space," Brice said. He placed a kiss on her cheek, then walked over to the door and opened it.

"Nice seeing you again, Ner—Nevealise," Langston said.

Nevealise chuckled as he caught himself. "You too, Langston. And for being such a gentleman, you can call me Nerd Girl for as long as you want. No offense taken." She grinned. "If you aren't comfortable with that name, my friends call me Nev."

"Thank you, Nev. See you on Sunday." Langston flashed his pearly whites again.

"What can I call you?" Jarred asked.

"I don't know. However, I have a few choice names I want to call you," she retorted.

"Fair enough. I apologize for my earlier assumptions. There, is that better?"

"I don't know, is it? How do you feel?"

Nevealise heard Brice and Langston snickering in the background. Her eyes were still fixed on Jarred.

He cast a glance over his shoulder at his brothers. "I'll meet you two outside," Jarred murmured.

"Why?" Brice asked.

"I just want a word. I believe we got off on the wrong foot and I want to set it straight," he responded.

Nevealise noticed Brice's eyes seesaw between her and Jarred. She felt the change in the atmosphere. There was tension, but not the angry, frustrated strain that was present before.

Jarred turned back to her. His stare was bold and presumptuous, but she felt drawn to him. She hadn't seen him since she was a teenager, so why was he affecting her in this way?

Nevealise didn't like it. At all. On stage she was bold and vivacious. She was Nev. However, offstage she was nerdy Nevealise, who liked numbers and playing on her computer. She was not comfortable with how Jarred made her feel.

"Come on, Brice. Jarred needs to apologize for acting like an ass," Langston said. "Honestly, I think he's met his match."

Nevealise watched as Brice reluctantly walked out the door, Langston right behind him, and closed it after them. Her heart raced uncontrollably as she turned to face Jarred. He had this look on his face, a look that clearly said he wanted her.

He walked over and stood in front of her.

"So you never told me what name to call you," he smirked. The handsome devil knew he was getting to her. Nevealise's breath hitched in her throat as he reached out, grabbed a lock of her hair and twirled the curly strand between his fingers. "Still no answer."

Nevealise cleared her throat. "Nevealise. You can call me Nevealise," she whispered.

"Nah, I don't think so." He gazed into her eyes.

"Nev then," she murmured, and tried to back up a little, but his arm snaked out and pulled her closer to him.

"How about I make up my own name for you? I like Nevea. How about you?" he whispered.

"Whatever works for you. Listen, I have to change," she breathed.

"Are you finished for the night?"

"Like I said before, maybe, maybe not."

"Have it your way. See you on Sunday, Nevea." He released her hair and then leaned down and brushed his lips across hers.

Then he simply turned and walked out, leaving her standing in the middle of the room staring at the closed door.

"Well, alrighty then," she said to the empty room. But her lips lifted in a slow smile.

Jarred walked out of the club and met his brothers.

"That meeting on Sunday has been shifted to my place. Call her tomorrow to inform her of the change," Jarred told Brice as they walked toward their cars.

"Do I look like your secretary? Why can't you call her?" Brice snorted.

"I don't remember what my secretary looks like, Brice, since you messed with her head and she took leave. And I can't call Nevea and change the venue because you and I both know she wouldn't come."

"So what makes you think she'd come if I ask her?"

"She seems to like you," Jarred grunted.

"She'd like you, too, if you weren't so grumpy." Langston chuckled.

"You seem to be all giggly tonight, Lang. What in the all-out hell is so funny?" Jarred demanded.

"You are, brother. You've pissed Nerd Girl off, and now she won't come out and play with you," Langston teased.

"She was steamed at him. I thought she was going to hit him at one point. Never seen Nev that mad before," Brice taunted.

"For one thing, dogs get mad, people get angry," Jarred said.

"And if she were a dog, she would have bit you on your arse," Brice countered. He was doubled over with laughter.

Evidently, his brothers found him funny, since they were both laughing like hyenas. But they weren't there to witness his and Nevea's sizzling exchange when they were alone. He'd leave the two knuckleheads with their assumptions. Suddenly, things seemed a whole lot brighter.

But Langston would not be deterred. "I distinctly remember you saying before we left the office that you didn't want to be around any 'touchy-feely' people. Yet there you were, trying to take Nev's hand with you," he joked.

Jarred needed to shut these two up quickly. He had

a feeling he'd be seeing a lot more of Ms. Nevealise Tempest. A whole lot more. Had he driven himself, he would have stayed longer, and left Langston and Brice to their own devices. Besides, wasn't that the point of their outing? To relax, have fun and enjoy the company of a beautiful woman? His brothers were still ribbing him. They were having just a little too much fun at his expense. His lips lifted in a slow smile. *Let's see who has the last laugh.*

"Be that as it may," he said, "who's coming in to work tomorrow? We still have a lot to do before the meeting next month with the board of directors." Jarred smiled at their collective grunts. *Ha! Who's laughing now?* They reached the cars. "Y'all want to grab a bite to eat at one of those all-night diners?" he asked.

"Sure," Langston said.

"Count me out. I have a few things to take care of. You two know how to get out of here, right?" Brice said.

"Of course we do," Langston responded.

"You okay, Brice?" Jarred asked.

"Good as gold." His remote started the car, but before he got in, he turned back to Jarred. "Since you apparently have the hots for Nev, I take it you want this meeting to be private. That being said, I will see you two at the office on Monday. Maybe." Brice got into his car and drove off.

"Something's up with him," Jarred said.

"I believe so, too. He'll tell us when he's ready. Let's go get some grub," Langston said.

Jarred got in on the passenger side, put his head back and closed his eyes.

"I'll GPS the closest diner," he heard Langston say, but his thoughts were still on Nevea. He found himself willing Sunday to come fast.

Chapter 4

Jarred lay in his king-size bed and looked over at the bedside clock. Six in the morning. He'd gotten very little sleep last night, and the night before. Usually, it was the trials of the office that kept him awake at night, but not this time. No, this time it was something sexy and tantalizing. Nevealise Tempest. Ever since he'd laid eyes on her Friday night, Jarred hadn't been able to get her off his mind.

She didn't know it, but he'd gone back to the club on Saturday, sat in the back away from the stage and watched her work her magic with the crowd. Jarred was surprised that she hadn't made it big in the music industry. She was just that good. According to Norman, people came from all over to see her perform, but she wasn't interested in the fame. She just loved singing and the atmosphere of Heavens. Norman had gone on to say that everyone in the club was surprised that she hadn't been around for almost a year, and then suddenly, two months ago, she'd appeared out of the blue, better than ever.

"What kept you away from the place you so obviously love, Nevea?" he asked in the semidarkened bedroom.

Jarred pushed the covers off and swung his legs over the bed, his bare feet touching the floor. He walked to the bureau, grabbed a pair of gym shorts and pulled them on over his boxer briefs. Then he put on a pair of socks and his sneakers and went into his en suite bathroom, where he washed his face and brushed his teeth. Jarred quickly grabbed his cell phone and then made his way to his basement, which housed his basketball court and gym.

Jarred went through a few warm-up drills before grabbing his basketball and running up and down the court, shooting baskets. Basketball was his game in high school and in college. He still loved the sport and played as much as he could. Not being able to get out to play with the fellas because of his demanding hours, he'd had his basement renovated into a full court.

He played for about an hour and a half before finally stopping and sitting on the floor, his back against the padded wall, his breathing heavy. He'd needed that workout.

"Oh, man. Jarred, either you're getting old or you need to get back in shape," he groaned, his arms on his knees and his head bowed, trying to suck in as much air as he could. Pushing up off the floor, he walked over to the bench where he'd placed his cell phone, and left the gym.

Brice hadn't phoned yet to say if Nevea was in fact coming, so it was basically a waiting game. An impatient waiting game. Jarred made his way to the master bathroom, showered, then dressed in sweatpants and a T-shirt from his alma mater, Howard University.

Next he needed a cup of coffee. Just as he was leaving his room, his cell phone chimed. He rushed to grab it from the bureau and looked at the caller ID. It was Brice.

"Man, you owe me big time and I plan to collect soon," his brother said.

"She's coming?"

"Yes. What did you say to her? I had a time convincing her to come to your house. She'll be there between ten thirty and eleven thirty." Brice laughed. "Or more likely by one thirty."

"What kind of timing is that?" Jarred frowned.

"Nev is as smart as a whip, but she gets lost going around the corner. She thinks she's smarter than the navigation system and gets lost every time."

It was Jarred's turn to chuckle. "I guess I won't make the eggs until she actually shows up at the door. From what you're saying, I may be making burgers, anyway. Why doesn't she take the train in and I'll pick her up from the station?"

"That would be a negative, brother. She would have to take the train into Penn and then the subway to Brooklyn. There is no way I'd trust Nev on the subway by herself."

"And you trust her to drive here?"

"She's a good driver. Her problem is unless she's singing, Nev always thinks in numbers. She tries to calculate everything. She's not familiar with Brooklyn.

Remember, like us, she grew up on Long Island. There are a lot of one-way streets in the five boroughs. Trust me, she'll calculate herself up in Albany somewhere."

"Damn." Jarred was laughing full out now. "How am I supposed to know if she's lost?"

"I gave her your cell number. I doubt she'll use it, so you take hers."

Jarred walked over to his nightstand and took out a notepad and pen. "Go ahead." He wrote down the digits as swiftly as Brice called them out.

There was a lot of rustling in the background on Brice's end, and then what sounded like a voice or voices.

"What's that noise?" Jarred raised a brow.

"No worries, brother. Talk to you soon. Tell Nev don't be too mad at me. Bye," Brice said, and disconnected the call.

Jarred stared down at his phone as if willing Brice to come through it so he could choke him.

"You keep hanging up on me, little brother, and I'm going to have to teach you some manners by going upside your lopsided head," Jarred said.

He went into the kitchen to get the coffeepot started. While he waited, he grabbed the remote control and turned the television on to watch the highlights of last night's basketball games.

Jarred went to the fridge and poured himself a glass of juice, downing it almost in one gulp. He was on his third cup of coffee and into the replay of the Knicks game when he heard his doorbell ring. It was 9:40 a.m. on a Sunday. *Who could that be this time of morning?* he thought, getting up to check. He looked through the peephole, then unlocked and opened the door.

"Nevea?" She was standing there wringing her hands. She looked like the nerd girl he'd often called her. Gone was the classy look from last night. Her hair pinned up in a fluffy ponytail, a white blouse was tucked into ripped jeans and a lightweight jacket. Complete with a pair of silver framed wire-rim glasses. Not as chic as she was at the club, but still just as beautiful. The schoolmarm look fit her personality perfectly. *She's mine. All day every day.*

"Brice did say the meeting had changed to your place."

"Yes. Yes. Come on in," he said, standing to the side to allow her to enter. "Brice said you would be here between ten thirty and eleven thirty."

"Knowing Brice, he said I would be here even later than that," she replied. "I'm not too early, am I?"

"No, of course not. Come on in and have a seat." He led her to the living room, where she sat on the sofa. "Would you like a cup of coffee?"

"Sure."

"How do you take it?"

"Milk, no sugar. I know I'm early, but what time are Brice and Langston due here?"

"Shortly," Jarred lied, taking a cup and saucer from the cupboard. "I'm gathering you found the place without a hitch."

"Almost. I was turned around a little bit."

"Oh yeah? Where'd you get turned around at?"

"Uh, Kingsbridge," she muttered.

"Huh? Did you say Kingsbridge?"

"Yes."

"Nevea, Kingsbridge is in the Bronx. I live in Brooklyn."

"I know that now, Jarred," she snickered.

Jarred didn't know whether to laugh at her or hug her. He decided not to do either.

"You still got here pretty early considering you not too long ago spoke to Brice."

"I was already on the road when I spoke to him again. He called me last night with the change of venue. I guessed he was checking up on me this morning."

"Just how long have you been driving?" Jarred asked, handing her a cup of coffee.

"A few hours."

"Why didn't you have myself, Brice or Langston pick you up?"

"I mapped the directions out to the letter. I must have missed a turn somewhere." Her brows furrowed as if she was in serious thought.

More like several turns. "Yes, that was probably it. You missed a turn somewhere," Jarred said, and sipped his coffee to keep from laughing. "Are you hungry? I'm starved."

"A little. I didn't eat yet. Besides, this is supposed to be a brunch. Yet I don't see or smell any food."

"My fault. You can bring that cup into the kitchen and sit at the island while I put something together. Unless you want to help."

"I'm sorry, but I'm not much of a cook," she said, following him into the kitchen.

"No worries. I got this. You like eggs, bacon, waffles, toast, sausages?"

"Yes, but not all at once."

"I'll tell you what. I'll cook and you eat whatever it is you want. How's that?"

"Sounds good to me. Shouldn't we wait for Brice and Langston?"

"No," he said, starting to take out the ingredients he needed.

Jarred worked effortlessly on their meal. When he was done, he placed all the dishes buffet-style on the island, and took out cutlery. "Have at it."

"Wow, this looks great," Nevealise said, and began to pile some of everything on her plate.

"Umm-hmm, it tastes good, too." He smiled, then frowned when he looked at her plate. "Are you going to eat all of that?"

"I sure am. Brice and Langston better hurry up and get here or they aren't going to have any food," she said.

"Don't worry about them. They aren't coming," he stated smoothly, before putting a forkful of eggs into his mouth.

"Wh-what do you mean, they aren't coming?"

"I asked them not to because I wanted to spend some time alone with you. To get to know you better. As I said before, we started out on the wrong foot." He shrugged. "Well, I didn't tell them I wanted alone time with you, but that is what I wanted."

"So you got me here on false pretenses? I don't like being manipulated, Jarred," she snapped, and stood up.

"You are not here on false pretenses. I plan to tell you everything that's going on. I just wanted to get to know you better in the process. Finish eating your food. You have nothing to fear from me, Nevea."

"I'm not afraid of you, Jarred. I'm annoyed with you for manipulating me. There's a difference."

Jarred watched Nevea intently as she moved food around on her plate with her fork, and then suddenly, as if she didn't have a care in the world, start demolishing it. His eyes bulged when she added more food to the almost-empty plate.

"When's the last time you ate?" he asked, his head bobbing to the rhythm of her fork going up and down.

"Sometime last night, I believe. No, wait—it was yesterday afternoon. I had a burrito and then some chips later on," she said around a mouthful of food.

"Yesterday! You only ate a burrito and some chips the whole day?"

"Right. Mmm, this is so delicious." She moaned and closed her eyes.

"Please, help yourself to everything that's left," he choked out. Her moans of delight caused a stirring in his loins.

"You know what would have been great with all of this?"

Watching her eat and listening to all the cooing sounds she was making turned him on. Nevea was eating as if she were in the throes of passion. "Sex," he said under his breath.

"Excuse me?"

He looked into her eyes and feigned innocence. "What?"

"You were mumbling something and I couldn't hear you," Nevea said.

"I'm sorry. You asked what would have been great with breakfast and I asked what?" he lied.

"Homemade home fries!" she said excitedly. "I love them with onions and peppers. They're to die for. My mom used to make them for me all the time."

"When was the last time you saw your parents?" Jarred noticed that Nevealise went from relaxed and eagerly eating to tightening up like a bow in zero-point-three seconds. Obviously, her parents were a touchy subject. He would stay away from any parent talk for now. "You don't have to answer if you don't want to."

"It's been a little while. I talk to my mom on the phone all the time, and my brothers check up on me at least once a month," she said with a half smile.

Her father. There was no mention of her being in contact with him. Jarred would leave that alone for now, as well. Instead, he stood up to take his dish to the sink.

"You want me to help?" she asked.

"Are you finished eating?" He raised his eyebrows and a smile curled his lips.

"I did eat a lot, didn't I?" She returned his smile.

"I would say you did. Yes." He chuckled. "No worries. I'm just happy you enjoyed the food."

"I'll help clean up." She got up from the bar stool and walked over to the sink.

"Cool. We can put everything in the dishwasher."

They worked side by side, with Jarred rinsing the plates and Nevealise loading the machine. He chuckled to himself. It was clear that Nevea was totally clueless in the kitchen, judging by the lost look on her face. And the fact that she was taking her cues from him. She would watch what he did and then mimic his actions. Well, she did say that she didn't know how to cook. How in the world did she manage on her own?

"There. All done," Jarred said. His cell phone buzzed on the counter just then. "Excuse me," he said, and rushed over to answer it. Looking down at the caller ID, he groaned inwardly. Langston. No doubt Brice had called him. *Bad timing, brothers.*

"Yes," Jarred all but snarled into the receiver.

"Whoa! What's gotten you all riled up? Your guest didn't show?"

Jarred could picture the smirk on his brother's face right now. And from the happy chirp of his voice, Langston sounded pleased that Nevea didn't show. He almost hated to burst his brother's bubble. Not really.

"On the contrary, my guest is here and you're an unwanted interruption," Jarred whispered.

"Really? You mean she actually showed?"

Jarred smiled at the surprise he heard in his brother's voice.

"Langston, I know you've spoken to Brice."

"No, I haven't. I called and didn't get an answer."

"Yes, she's here. I have to go. Bye," he murmured, and abruptly disconnected the call.

Jarred didn't have time for small talk with his brother. He needed to get to Nevea before she found an excuse to leave. He turned his cell off and went in search of her.

Chapter 5

Nevealise took a tour of Jarred's home while he talked on the phone. The two-story brownstone was a big house for one person. His kitchen was long and rectangular, with a center island that could seat at least eight people. Standing there, she looked past a few columns out into the living area. Everything on this floor looked new, so it had to have been recently renovated. Modern with old-style charm.

Completing the first floor was a formal dining room that was closed off by double sliding doors that could clearly be mistaken for part of the kitchen wall. Nevealise smiled inwardly. Nice touch. That small detail maintained the old charm of the home.

She walked around a long dining table, cherrywood highlighted by ornate carvings. The elegant gold tipping and expensively upholstered chairs surrounding the table gave the room a regal look.

"I thought I'd lost you," Jarred's smooth voice teased from across the room.

She started. Her eyes darted to where he stood, and honed in on his broad chest with the words Howard University printed across the front of the fitted T-shirt. Her gaze shifted to the sweatpants he wore, to his slippers, and then traveled back up to his face, where he wore a mile-wide smile. Nevealise could feel the blush starting at her neck and creeping across her cheeks. She lowered her head.

"I take it you like what you see," he said, and she couldn't help but let her eyes meet his. Her face was now several shades of red, and she knew it.

"What?" she choked out.

"The house—you like what you've seen so far?" He smirked.

They both knew that he wasn't talking about his house. Nevealise walked past him, or tried to, anyway. He blocked her exit.

"I like the house just fine from what I've seen of it," she said haughtily. "Excuse me."

"After you, milady." He bowed and laughed. "Come on, I'll give you a guided tour of the rest of the place." He took her hand in his, pulling her alongside him.

"Why do you have such a huge home for one person?"

"I don't know. At first it was for entertainment purposes, but I use my home in the Hamptons for the little entertaining that I do now. I put in so many hours at the office that I'm rarely here." He looked around. "It's a waste, really," he said.

Nevealise heard pain in his voice. She wondered what wound she'd opened up, and then it hit her. Brice had mentioned that Jarred had been engaged to be married a few years ago, and that the wedding had been called off. He hadn't given her any details. Now she wondered what really happened, and if this house was in some way a part of the pain that she'd heard in his voice.

"A rather expensive waste, wouldn't you agree?" she teased, flashing him a smile.

"Very." He grinned.

"I'm sure you had your reasons for purchasing it. In any event, it's stunning and not overly stated. Very homey, with a warm and cozy feel. Guests are not made to feel afraid to sit or touch anything for fear of messing something up or breaking your valuables. Very comfy."

"A house is made to be lived in, not looked at and admired from afar. I guess that's why there's a difference between a house and a home. A home is lived in. Welcome to my home, Nevea."

"Thanks for having me, Jarred."

"From your comments, I take it that you've broken a few pieces here and there at someone's home?" he teased.

"Of course I have. Ballet and other dance classes have helped some with my clumsiness. However, when I'm into my work I have been known to walk into things and knock stuff over. If I'm not wearing my contacts or glasses, forget about it. I'm a total klutz."

"Well, everything in here is replaceable, so no worries. As long as you don't hurt yourself, have at it." He chuckled. "Let's get started with that tour. We'll start with the lower level—the basement." He opened the door and walked down the steps. Nevea followed.

"Wow, you've turned your basement into a basketball court. Nice. This must have been a big renovation project." She looked around the spacious area at the wall-to-wall padding. Aside from the court there was a workout area, which included a weight bench, dumbbells and a boxing bag at the far end.

"You like basketball?"

"It's okay. I used to watch my brothers and their friends play. I can live with or without it." She shrugged.

"You know it's funny. Your father and mine are close buddies, yet our families never interacted much. Actually, until you showed up to tutor my sister, I had forgotten Mr. Tempest even had children. Why's that? I find it rather odd," he said softly.

"Hmm, that is odd, isn't it?" she said quietly, not offering up any additional information. "I believe we hung out more when we were all younger, and let's face it. You're older than I am, so you wouldn't have noticed me too much, anyway. Or it could have just been that your father grew tired of Josiah Tempest."

"You really don't care for your father, do you?"

"I'd rather not talk about it." She wouldn't tell Jarred that the man who claimed to be good friends with his father was well and truly a pompous, male-chauvinist pig who treated Nevealise and her mother like the hired help rather than a daughter and a wife. The one time Nevealise had thought she'd earned her father's respect, it had turned out to be a lie. He'd used her, too. Just like he'd used most people in his life.

Her father knew she'd wanted to be a part of the family business, but no, he wanted her brothers to join the company. To Josiah Tempest's chagrin both her brothers had gone to medical school instead. Then here came poor little awkward, bookwormish Nevealise.

Trying to please her daddy, she'd agreed to help him install special security software and several other high profile programs that she'd created herself for the mortgage company's computers. She'd done so with the assurance that she would oversee not only the implementation of the programs, but also be given a managerial spot in the company alongside her father. Of course, that never happened. Just as soon as her programs were operational, her services were no longer needed, and at that very moment she'd realized that she didn't need her father, nor did she want anything to do with him. So she stayed away.

"So-o-o, would you rather play some one-on-one?"

"What?" She arched a brow. Nevealise had been so engrossed in her thoughts that she hadn't heard a word Jarred said.

"Basketball. Would you like to play a game?"

"I haven't played in a while. My brothers used to make me participate to even out the players when they had a few friends over. Frankly, I would have rather been reading a book."

"Both your brothers are doctors, correct?"

"Yes, they are." She smiled.

"I take it you're on good terms with them?"

"Of course I am. Why wouldn't I be?"

"No reason other than the fact that every time I mention anything about your family you clam up."

"Not true. I just don't talk about my father."

"You never answered my question," Jarred said. "Do you want to play a game of B-ball?"

He picked up the basketball. His muscles flexed, causing her mouth to practically drop open. Jarred was all man. A handsome man full of sex appeal. After all these years, he still had an effect on her hormones. Nevealise couldn't deal with being up close and personal with him in a game of one-on-one. Not with the way her body was reacting to his mere presence. Instead of agreeing to the game, she took the cowardly way out.

"Maybe. I'd like to see the rest of the house first. If you don't mind."

"Sure. Come on." He threw the ball down, took her hand and led her back up the stairs.

With her senses already heightened, the warmth of his hand against hers had her tingling all over. So much so that she couldn't keep from shivering a bit. Her body's reaction to his was foreign. Sure, Nevealise had crushed on him for a long time, but this…this need was so strong it scared her.

Oh man, oh man, she chanted over and over in her head. *I am so in trouble.* Her body was betraying her big time. A chill coursed through her, causing her to shiver again.

"You cold?" he asked.

"Not at all. What's on the top floor?" she asked, changing the subject.

"Be patient. I'm about to show you." He laughed.

"Yes, but you're being slow about it," she joshed. "You know you're going to have to let go of my hand in order for me to walk up the stairs."

"No, I don't."

"Yes, you do," she said, breathing in his manly scent mixed with what may have been Irish Spring soap. Nevealise was proved right when they couldn't walk side by side up the steps. Jarred quickly remedied the situation by taking hold of her opposite hand. She had to walk slightly behind him, but not much.

"I told you so." He looked back at her and smirked.

Before she could react to having his body so close to hers, he went into tour guide mode. "There are four bedrooms up here," he told her, "including the master suite, three additional rooms and a full bath. Two of the rooms are used as guest rooms and the other I made into a den/office/library. Here, let me show you," he said, walking past two rooms on the right to get to a third one. He opened the door to a large space. Built-in shelves lined the walls, filled with books and hundreds of DVDs. There were also a leather sofa, a desk and a full entertainment center.

"How'd you manage this, and so comfortable, too? Confess. You had a decorator, right?"

"I sure did and I am proud of it. The decorator did a fantastic job throughout the house. Not too manly or girlie. It's just right."

"This is lovely. I love the natural lighting from the skylights. I don't know how you get any work done in here. I'd surely fall asleep from the warm and cozy feel of the room. So much harmony and balance." She sighed, closed her eyes and breathed in and out.

"I'm glad you like it. Feel free to stop by and take advantage of it anytime you like," he said softly. There was a husky catch in his voice. She opened her eyes and glanced over to where he stood next to the doorway. The look on his face couldn't mask the desire she saw in his eyes.

Nevealise wasn't overly experienced where the opposite sex was concerned. She had never really had a serious relationship. Her only sexual partner had been a fellow college student, and sex between them was more an experiment than actual lovemaking. She wasn't even sure they'd done it right. He'd lasted a minute—a whole minute of him huffing and puffing and blowing his hot breath on her. They couldn't even kiss properly because his braces kept clicking against her teeth. When it was over, he was saying how great it was, but the only thing she'd felt was pain. Nothing else. Thank goodness they'd had the sense to use a condom.

Everything Nevealise knew about sex and how to please a partner, she'd learned from a book and online research. Some of the things she read about still had her blushing.

Granted, she might not have experience, but she recognized what she wanted when she saw it. And Jarred wasn't hiding the fact that he wanted her.

Time to go.

Nevealise looked down at the slim watch on her wrist. Her eyes bulged. "It's well past noon! Oh my goodness, where'd the time go?" she cried.

Jarred stared at her. "Time flies when you're having fun," he said hoarsely.

"I guess so," she said softly. "Listen, I need to get back. I have an early flight out tomorrow."

"Oh?" he inquired, one dark brow lifting.

"I have a job, remember? I'm a consultant, contracted out for our good ole government. NCIS, to be exact. I'm also in the process of designing my own video game. I travel all over for research and work."

Jarred whistled through his teeth. "Seems like you're carrying a heavy load. NCIS—isn't that military?"

"Yes, it is. However, I am not now and never was

in the military. I just help design stuff. In some sense you could say I'm a paid hacker." She laughed outright at the expression on Jarred's face, a mixture of surprise and shock.

"I would have never thought of you working for the military police. Especially since you got lost coming from Long Island to Brooklyn," he teased. "Seriously, I thought Heavens was your job."

"No, Heavens is my baby. It keeps me sane when my job becomes stressful. In any event, I need to get going." She tried to push past him. He wasn't having it.

"There's one room you still haven't seen." He didn't give her time to respond; he took her hand and guided her out of the room, stopping in front of the door opposite the library.

She knew where he was leading her. The only other room to her knowledge that was left to see. The master bedroom.

"And this is the master suite," he announced proudly, releasing her hand and opening the door.

Nevealise's feet moved of their own accord. Like a robot, she walked into the spacious bedroom, her eyes roaming the contents. Two wingback, tailored chairs and a small round table sat in front of a large picture window. Opposite the window was an open doorway, and next to that a huge four-poster bed with distinctive carvings. The bureau and nightstands had some of the same ornate carvings, but the bed was the focal point of the room.

Nevealise was in such awe of the breathtaking space that she didn't notice Jarred standing behind her until she felt his arms encircling her, pulling her back against his rock-hard frame.

"You like?" he whispered huskily in her ear. The warmth of his breath sent tingling sensations down her spine and straight to her center. Her thighs clenched as if to stem the desire coursing through her.

"It's simply gorgeous. I feel compelled to take off my shoes upon entering," she croaked. She could feel his manhood growing against her butt and her breathing accelerated, along with her heartbeat.

"This is my sanctuary," he murmured against her ear. "In this room, in that bed, is where I hope to make all of my babies, while making love to the one woman who will bear my children. Making love to her over and over and over again will be my pleasure, while taking her to sexual heights she never would've imagined in her wildest dreams. How does that sound, Nevea?" he whispered.

"Wh-why are you asking me?" she choked out. Nevealise felt his stomach shaking against her back and realized that he was laughing.

"You'll figure it out soon enough," he said. He leaned forward and nipped her on her neck.

"Ouch! What did you do that for?" she cried, turning in his arms to face him. Uh-oh. Bad move. The next thing Nevealise felt were his lips on hers, and he was kissing her soundly. His manhood, nestled against the apex of her thighs, had her mind wrestling with the idea of moving against him. But before she could decide, he abruptly ended the kiss.

"Sweetheart, if you don't want to find yourself stripped naked in that bed over there, legs spread wide with me between your thighs, this tour has now come to an end," he breathed.

"Okay." It was the only thing she could mutter as she tried to get air into her lungs.

"If you have time, we could go for a walk before you have to leave. I don't want our visit to end. However, we need to get out of this house before I do something you'll regret later on. So how about a brisk walk through the neighborhood?"

"Sure. Why not? You still haven't told me why I'm here in the first place."

"Yes, I did. You're here because I want you here. Simple as that."

"No, you and your brothers wanted to discuss something with me. Remember?"

"Another time. Let me grab a jacket and my kicks, and we can leave." He released her, then disappeared into the walk-in closet and emerged with a hoodie and a pair of sneakers in his hand. After putting on both, he grabbed her shaky hand and they left the room.

Chapter 6

Jarred sat frustrated at his desk. He was on his fourth conference call and it wasn't even noon.

"Basically, Jarred, we need to get into this locked computer. I have tried everything and nothing will break it. There's some kind of software and hardware that I've never seen before. Whoever installed it is a genius and we need them on our side pronto," Emerson, his IT guy, was saying.

"And the answers we need are locked in this computer?" Jarred asked.

"I believe so. Yes," Emerson responded.

"My question is how do we know that what we need is on this computer if we can't get into it?" Jarred asked. His voice sounded like he felt: exasperated.

He was exasperated with the entire mess that was Tempest Mortgage, as well as not being able to reach Nevea. He didn't know why she wasn't returning his

calls. They'd parted on what he thought were good
terms. After their walk, he'd convinced her to have
lunch with him. They'd gone back to the house and
he'd ordered their meal from a local Mexican restau-
rant that he frequented.

After lunch he'd walked her to her car, parked
two blocks away, had checked her GPS to make sure
she had it programmed correctly and had even programmed directions into her cell phone. "Use both
just in case," he'd said with a smile, after kissing her
thoroughly.

That had been almost a week ago. And he hadn't
heard from her since.

He hadn't dared broach the subject of Tempest Mortgage that afternoon, nor of her father, not wanting to
ruin the good time they were having. Maybe he should
have seen that the outcome might be the same.

As far as he could tell she wasn't aware that Manning Enterprises had acquired her father's failing company.

"So where the hell is she?" Jarred grumbled.

"What's that?" he heard Emerson say. The man
sounded confused.

Join the club.

"Nothing, Emerson." He shook his mind clear of its
ramblings and focused on the problem his IT guy had
presented. "What were you saying about the computer?
I apologize. I got distracted for a minute. This one little bitty company is going to send me over the edge."

"I was saying we don't know this information is
there. However, it would help to get into the computer,
if for nothing else than to see what Tempest was trying to hide."

"Maybe it's nothing. The old man could have just been particular about his company."

"I don't think so. This computer and several others were the main ones in the accounting department, as well as business services, IT and security. Boss, you know what I used to do and who I used to be. No, I'm telling you—you do not go to these lengths for no reason. Either the old man had something to hide or he was protecting someone or several people," Emerson responded.

Jarred had to agree with him. Something was going on. Throwing his pen on his desk, he sat back in his chair and folded his hands behind his head. A move he'd been doing a lot of lately. However, he needed to think, and this was as good as it got at the moment.

"Have you spoken to Brice?" Jarred asked.

"I spoke to him a few days ago. He feels the same as I do. That upper management at Tempest was hiding something."

"I pray not all of them. Most of them are working for other companies now. Maybe the senior VPs. They would have access to a lot of information."

"True. From what I have gathered this was probably put in place after Tempest started its sudden fall from grace. The question is why?"

Jarred listened to Emerson. He liked this man's thought process, having learned over the years to trust his opinions. Jarred had known Emerson ever since the IT specialist had gone to school with Langston. Despite being a bright young man, he'd left college in his junior year, married his high school sweetheart and then went off to the military after finding out his wife was pregnant. Upon his return from his stint in the service, he started working for his wife's family, and that was where his life took a downward turn. What Emerson thought was a successful group of people were nothing but glorified criminals. His ex-wife and her family members all went to prison. Fortunately, Emerson had gotten off on a technicality. He was left to raise their now ten-year-old daughter.

Emerson had a stellar military record, and the DA honestly believed he was not aware of his in-laws' actions, so decided not to pursue any further legal action against him. Still, his legal problems were big news and no one would hire him.

It was by chance that Jarred and his brothers had run into Emerson at a bar, getting wasted. He'd been too drunk to get behind the wheel of a car, so Jarred had driven him to his parents' home and given him a stern talking to. Two days later he found himself hiring Emerson as part of his IT team. The man was more than qualified and great at what he did. As had been shown by his military record, Emerson was a stellar employee. He was now working on his fifth year of employment with Manning Enterprises. It was definitely time for a promotion. Jarred would discuss it with his brothers.

"Hey, boss, you still there?"

"I'm still here. Listen, get together with the security team and have a discussion with them about our current situation. See if they feel the same as you and I. Also, are you available for a meeting…say, Monday morning first thing?"

"I'll make the time. How's nine thirty?"

"That'll be fine. If you and Security come up with anything in the meantime, let me or my brothers know immediately. And do me a favor. Don't let anyone know what we're doing. Remember, we have a lot of Tempest employees working for us. If there's some funny business going on I don't want to tip our hand. I want the person gone."

"Gotcha. Will do, boss."

"And will you please stop calling me boss," Jarred snapped. "It's annoying as hell and you know it."

"Whatever you say...boss," Emerson mocked. Jarred could hear the humor in his voice.

He stifled a laugh, a testament to the easy camaraderie he had with the employee who was more like a brother to him. "Goodbye, Emerson. This meeting is over. If you see Brice hanging about, tell him to stop by my office."

"He's walking toward me now. I'll give him your message. Talk to you later, Jarred."

Jarred disconnected the conference call and immediately picked up his cell from his desk and dialed Nevea's number.

"Hello, you have reached—"

"Voice mail," he barked, hanging up the phone and tossing it across his desk. With the amount of paperwork that was on his desktop the cell was safe. He stared at the phone a few minutes more, then picked it up and dialed her again. Voice mail. "Where the hell are you, Nevea?"

There was a knock on his office door, but before he could ask who it was, the door was pushed open and in walked Brice, with Langston on his heels.

"What do you two want?" he growled.

"I was summoned," Brice replied, his tone sarcastic.

"I was on my way to see Brice when he was on his

way up here to see you." Langston shrugged. "What's wrong with you?"

"Nothing," he snarled, rummaging through the stack of files on his desk, pretending to be looking for something. In fact, Jarred had no idea what he was doing. He was angry with Nevea for not returning his calls and angrier at himself for giving a damn. He should have learned his lesson from Lainey, but no, he had to go get heated over Nevea.

"You rang?" Brice barked.

"Cut the crap, Brice. I'm not in the mood," Jarred snapped.

"Well, why'd you ask me to come see you if you knew your disposition sucked?" Brice asked, throwing up his hands.

Jarred noticed Langston had taken a seat in one of the chairs in front of his desk, a grin on his face. What was *he* smirking about?

Brice was right; he shouldn't be taking his anger out on them. With a heavy sigh, Jarred relented. "Sorry," he mumbled.

"What was that? I couldn't hear you," Brice said, holding his hand to his ear.

"Don't push your luck, little brother. Have a seat," Jarred growled. "Has Emerson made you aware of his thoughts on the computer problem?" he asked, already knowing the answer.

"Yes, he has, and I am in agreement with him," Brice said, with a nod.

"Well, can you two bring me up to speed?" Langston interjected.

Jarred went on to tell him about the conversation

he'd had with Emerson, ending with the computer genius's suppositions.

"That would make sense, considering what I've just learned," Langston said.

Jarred sat up straighter in his chair and stared at his brother. "What have you learned?" he and Brice asked almost simultaneously.

"Dad definitely didn't do his homework on this one. For one thing, Tempest has several settled lawsuits and one pending suit filed against them. Cases ranging from underwater mortgages to bribery. I'm compiling a list of complaints and I'll apprise you of the results after I'm done. Jarred, we're going to have to put our fancy law degrees to use in a big way in order to fix this mess at Tempest."

"We need to get this done quickly. Before the next board meeting for sure. I don't want anything getting out about Tempest until we can get a handle on things. We don't need our stock taking a hit because of this nightmare of a business we've inherited," Jarred groaned. He felt a king-size headache coming on.

"I told Dad not to invest in that company. I told him," Brice stormed.

"Yeah, yeah, Brice, we know. Too late now. We have to make the best of the cards we've been dealt. We need to handle this and move on," Jarred said.

"I agree." Langston chimed in. "Nothing we can do about it now. It's no longer Josiah Tempest's problem. It's ours. We have to be the ones to turn things around."

"And we're going to need all hands on deck to do that," Jarred replied. "However, I'm not trusting any of Tempest's employees. In light of the new information, we need thorough background checks on the employees that are working for us, and on anyone who was in a top position and no longer is with the company. As well as anyone who was abruptly fired from Tempest. The works."

Brice nodded. "I'll get with the security team, and do a little bit of research on my own, as well. I have a lot of contacts. I'll start with financials. However, we need to get into that computer."

"That's one of our top priorities, for sure. Getting into that computer may eliminate a few steps in this tedious process," Jarred said.

His cell began to chime. Instinctively, he grabbed it and answered. "Jarred Manning."

"Jarred?"

Nevea, he said to himself, and then swiveled his chair away from his brothers.

"Where are you?" he asked crisply.

"Working," she responded, her tone just as brisk. "Why, what do you want?"

"I've been going out of my mind with worry. You never phoned and haven't returned any of my calls," he said, a little calmer now.

"That's because I didn't have time. I'm working. I told you I would be catching a plane out the next morning when we were together Sunday. So what's the problem?"

Jarred ran his hand across his face. He needed to calm down before he said something he'd regret later on. From the tone of her voice she was already teed off with him. He couldn't understand why she was being snippy. She was the one not returning calls. However, he did remember her saying she'd be flying out. He'd just forgotten about it.

"Yeah, you did." He sighed heavily.

"Listen, I need to catch at least an hour's nap before I have to get back to work."

"It's almost quitting time and you're going back to work?" he questioned, and was glad she couldn't see his scowl.

"Not here. It's a little after four in the morning in my time zone."

"Just where are you?" he asked, his scowl deepening.

"Japan."

Jarred swallowed hard. What in the world was she doing in Japan, and just what business did she have there? Was it part of her work as a consultant for NCIS? These were all questions that would have to wait for answers until she returned.

"When do you come home?" he found himself asking.

"I don't know, Jarred. When the job is done. Hopefully soon. I'm worn-out. My body hasn't really adjusted to the time change yet." As if to underscore what she said, she yawned.

"Are you eating properly?"

"No. I don't have time to worry about it," she responded. Jarred could hear the tiredness in her voice.

"We're going to have a conversation about that when you get back. Rest. Call me when you can," he whispered.

"I'll try. Talk to you soon, Jarred. Bye."

"Talk to you soon, love," he said, and smiled to himself as he disconnected the call. He could have sworn he heard a smile in her voice, too. He made a mental note to look up the time zone difference and text her three times a day to remind her to eat and rest. Hopefully, she'd actually see the text. She was bound to see one, if not all.

Jarred's smile was broad as he swung his chair back around—only to come face-to-face with his brothers. *Ah, hell.* He'd forgotten that they were still in his office. The smirks they both sported were telltale signs that they'd been listening to his conversation.

"What?" he asked, playing dumb. He was not going to tell them he was talking to Nevea. Nope. His love life, or lack thereof, was none of their business.

"Well, well, well, I do believe our brother has gone and found himself a woman," Langston said.

"It's about time," Brice added. "Moaning and groaning over Lainey was working my last nerve. So who is she?"

"I have no idea what you two are talking about. Now get out of my office. We all have work to do."

Brice and Langston's collective bellyaching put a smile on Jarred's face. *That'll teach them a lesson for trying to get into my personal affairs,* Jarred thought.

"Oh, I forgot. I asked Emerson to meet with us on Monday morning," he called out to the retreating duo.

"For what?" Langston asked.

"I want to promote him to head of Security. He deserves it. He's practically running the security and IT departments as it is. He may as well get paid for it," Jarred said. "You agree?"

"Good move. He's a good man. The promotion is well deserved," Langston said.

"I don't have a problem with it. Like Langston said, Emerson's a good guy," Brice chimed in.

"Glad we're all in agreement. See you later," Jarred

said, and then picked up a folder. He didn't lift his head until his office door closed. Then he swiveled his chair around to face the window. He started as his door opened again and Brice peeked in.

"For the record, don't be too rough on Nev. She works hard and forgets to take care of herself. Tell her I said hello when she calls you back," Brice said confidently. Then he laughed and closed the door after him.

"His arrogance is annoying," Jarred said to the empty room.

Chapter 7

Nevealise opened her eyes in a haze of cotton webs, or at least that's what it felt like. She'd returned to Cambridge last night and had gone straight to her bed. Her comfortable bed, but most importantly, her own bed. But now someone was ringing her bell and pounding on her door. Grabbing her eyeglasses off the night table, she looked at her bedside clock. Five o'clock in the evening.

"Wow," she mumbled. She'd been sleeping for about fourteen hours straight, and she was still tired. The insistent pounding continued. After jumping up from the bed, Nevealise made her way to the door. "Who is it?" she called.

"Nevea, it's me, Jarred. Open up, love."

Why was he here? Better yet, how did he know where she lived? She unlocked and opened the door to a smiling Jarred.

"What in the world are you doing here?" she murmured sleepily. His smile vanished as he gave her a once-over.

"Nevea, I think you need to let me in. You're standing in the doorway in your underwear," he said huskily.

Nevealise looked down at herself, cried in horror and took off running to her bedroom, where she slipped on pajama pants and a tank top, and then quickly brushed her teeth. When she went back to find Jarred, he wasn't where she'd left him. He was in her kitchen, removing containers of food from two plastic grocery bags.

"What are you doing?" Nevealise asked.

"Feeding you. From the looks of it you've been starving yourself."

Nevealise smiled. From the day he found out that she was in Japan, a week ago, he'd texted her three times a day telling her to eat. A smiley face emoji always accompanied the text. She'd been able to call him only a couple times, but he'd phoned her twice a day, leaving her a good-morning and a good-night voice mail.

She took a seat at the breakfast nook. "How'd you know I hadn't eaten anything? I've been back since last night."

"I figured with the time zone difference you'd probably sleep the day away. I hadn't expected you to still be asleep," he chuckled.

"Yeah, but I told you I'd drive out to your place on Sunday. It takes a couple of days, sometimes more, for my body to adjust to time changes."

"I know you did, but I wanted to see you sooner. It's been two weeks, you know," he murmured, looking over at her.

"Almost two weeks. It would have been two weeks

on Sunday," she corrected him. "You know, no one's ever looked after me like you've been doing. I mean, not since I was in high school. It felt good," she whispered.

"Oh, come now. I know your parents and brothers checked on you," he teased.

"Sure, my mom and brothers, but they don't count. They're family."

"They still count. You need to eat," he said, turning the containers toward her. "We have baked chicken, veggies, mashed potatoes, sweet potatoes, rolls and corn bread. For dessert there's apple pie, blueberry pie and strawberry cheesecake. What do you want to start with, and where are your dishes?"

"Everything you need is in the cabinet across from you, and I'll have everything except for corn bread. Afterward, I'll have the apple pie for dessert." She eyed the food with longing. Just then her stomach betrayed her and growled. It was so loud that Nevealise was embarrassed.

"Tell your stomach to hold its horses. Your food is coming right up," he said with a chuckle as he started piling food on a plate. "Eat up," he added, when he brought it over to her.

"This looks scrumptious. Aren't you having any?" she asked, and scooped up a healthy helping of mashed potatoes with gravy.

"Yes, I am. Fixing my plate now," he said, and then snapped his fingers as if he'd forgotten something.

"What?"

"Drinks. Do you have anything?"

"There should be water, juice and sodas in the

fridge. I can't remember if I restocked." She frowned, biting on a piece of chicken.

He opened the refrigerator and barked her name. "Nevea!"

She startled. "What's wrong?" she asked hurriedly.

"You have a refrigerator full of energy drinks and nothing else," he said, sounding horrified.

"There's got to be more in there."

"Nevea, you have exactly two bottles of water, a container of orange juice that I am sure is expired, along with what looks like it could have been milk. The rest is multiple cans of energy drinks. You're going to kill yourself with that stuff," he said, chastising her. "I thought singers took better care of their voices?"

"Jarred, stop being so dramatic. Energy drinks are not dangerous at all." She shrugged. "They're my fuel for my all-nighters."

"And just how many of those do you have?"

"The drinks or the all-nighters?"

"Both."

"A lot."

"Nevea, energy drinks are intended to give you a boost, not to supplement meals or replace them," he said, grabbing two bottles of water and going to sit next to her at the breakfast nook. "Here, drink this. No more energy drinks for you while I'm here."

"I don't want two bottles of water. Besides, if I drink both of these, what are you going to drink?"

"I don't know. Do you have any alcohol in this place? I could use a stiff drink," he grunted.

"I may have a bottle of chardonnay hanging around," she said, getting up to go in search of it.

"Why am I not surprised? Girlie wine and energy

drinks. Don't bother. I'm not really a wine drinker. I'll have a bottle of water. Sit back down and eat," he said, digging into his food.

Nevealise shrugged, sat and began to consume the rest of her meal. Jarred kept piling extra food on her plate and she ate every bit like a champ.

"Wow, I was really hungry," she said, astounded at the amount of food she'd eaten.

"You were. This is what happens when you starve yourself. I would make a pot of coffee, but there isn't any milk. Is there a grocery store or something in the area?" Jarred asked.

"There's a delicatessen a few blocks away if milk's all you want," she said around a yawn. "There are plenty of grocery stores around here. I suggest staying local, since you don't know the area. Where'd you park?"

"In one of your spots. You did say you have two." When she gave him a puzzled look, he added, "You told me exactly where you lived. Do you remember any of our conversations? Never mind, go back to bed. You're dead on your feet. I'll take a ride to the store. Scratch that. I'll walk to a store. Give me your door key so I can let myself back inside," he said, holding his hand out.

"There should be a set on the table in the entryway. Grab those," she said. "I'm going to lie down. I'm sorry. So tired."

"You have nothing to apologize for. Go lie down. I'll be back shortly," he said, and walked over to place a kiss on her forehead.

Nevealise went back into her bedroom and climbed into bed. As soon as her head hit the pillow, she drifted off to sleep.

* * *

Jarred had returned from the store over an hour ago. He'd checked on Nevea. She was dead to the world. She must have been really tired. She hadn't stirred when he walked into her bedroom and placed a kiss on her head.

Nevealise's town house was really clean for someone who claimed she couldn't cook and was always on the go. Jarred had given himself a tour. Her place was more modern than his, with stainless steel appliances, marble countertops and hardwood floors throughout. The rooms didn't have a whole lot of furnishings, but they had a fresh lemony smell that actually suited her.

Jarred looked down at his watch. It was nine o'clock in the evening. He was sitting in her den watching television and listening to the bustling sounds from outside. His cell phone chimed and he answered.

"Jarred, where are you?" Langston's voice came through the earpiece.

"Out. Why?"

"You left the office early and no one has seen or heard from you. I was just wondering."

"I'm fine, Langston. I just needed to get away and clear my head for a bit."

"I hear you, man. I'm thinking of doing the same. I may go hang out in the Poconos for the weekend. If I didn't have any meetings tomorrow, I'd leave tonight."

"Cancel them and go," Jarred said.

"Wait a minute. You're not dying or something, are you, bro?"

"Not that I'm aware of," Jarred replied drily.

"Well, something's wrong if you're telling me to cancel meetings and take off."

"We've been killing ourselves for six months. At

the rate we're going, one or all of us will have a heart attack."

"I've had my yearly physical and according to my doctor I'm fit as a fiddle."

"Langston, my brother, stress kills, too."

"That is true. Listen, my secretary is peeking her head in my door." His brother's groan was heard through the telephone. "I'll see you bright and early tomorrow morning."

"Talk to you tomorrow." Jarred didn't tell him that he wouldn't be in the office. He planned on spending as much time as he could with Nevea, before his job and hers intruded again.

He put his cell phone away, kicked off his shoes and stretched out across the leather sofa. He'd rest up a bit before Nevea awakened. As soon as his eyes closed, he drifted off to sleep. At one point he glanced up briefly and thought he saw a cover or something being placed on him. Whatever it was, it was soft. He snuggled deeper into the warmth. "Thank you," he mumbled, and that was the last thing he remembered.

Chapter 8

Jarred came awake slowly. His eyes moved across the room as he tried to get his bearings. For a minute he was confused by his surroundings, and then it hit him: he was at Nevea's. He'd fallen asleep on the sofa in the den. He glanced down at the soft throw that covered him. So he hadn't imagined it. A slow smile began to inch across his lips.

Sitting up, he glanced at his watch and was stunned at the time. It was after eight in the morning. He'd never slept past six. At eight o'clock he'd have already been sitting behind his desk at work, and on his third cup of coffee.

"You're awake." A throaty voice came from the doorway.

Jarred swung his gaze in that direction. Nevealise stood in the open doorway. Her hair was in a dishev-

eled mess all over her head. Her natural beauty shone
as bright as the morning sun. She wore a pair of boxer-
type shorts and a long-sleeved shirt similar to the one
she'd worn at his house. Only this one fit her hand like
a half glove—her thumb sticking out through a slit in
the sleeve. In her hand was a coffee mug that she had
a death grip on, and she shifted nervously from one
foot to the other.

Why was she nervous? Was she feeling this pull,
this attraction that couldn't be contained? It had been
there from the very beginning and hadn't subsided. His
manhood began to throb and swell against his slacks.
He wanted her with a fierceness that couldn't be denied. His eyes bored into hers, almost daring her to
look away. The rise and fall of her chest was a sure
sign that she was just as aware of him as he was of her.

"Yes. I'm awake," he replied huskily. "I haven't slept
this late in a long time. It must be the company."

"There's coffee made if you want some," she murmured, and as she lowered her head, Jarred knew she
was trying to avoid direct eye contact with him.

"I sure do. Let me take a quick shower, if that's okay,
and I'll be right out."

She nodded. "You can use the bathroom down the
hall. I'll get you some fresh towels. I'm afraid I don't
have anything you can change into," she added. Jarred
caught the teasing tone and responded in kind.

Tilting his head to the side, he let his gaze travel
boldly up and down her body. "I don't have a problem
walking around in the buff. What say you? Would you
have an issue with me being nude?" he murmured,
never taking his eyes off her.

He watched her intently, practically making love to

her with his eyes. Her quick intake of breath, the slight shiver of her body and the glazing over of her eyes were not lost on him. To add fuel to the fire, Jarred licked his lips. A sound escaped her mouth, so decadent, so wanton Jarred almost lost his mind. His arousal went straight to the roof. He needed to stop this game he was playing before he was the one to get burned.

"I don't think that would be a good idea," she breathed.

"Why not? I rather like the idea myself," he crooned. She blushed beautifully. "No worries, my sweet Nevea. I have a small case that I usually keep in my trunk for emergency purposes. I brought it in last night and put it in your hall closet. I'll just grab it and get that shower."

He was so hard he dared not move just yet. Nevealise either sensed something or could tell he had an erection, because her eyes stretched as big as saucers and she bolted.

"Okay. I'll—I'll meet you in the kitchen," she said as she rushed out of the room.

Jarred wanted to laugh, but he was so hard it hurt. She would have surely made a run for it had she seen his erection protruding like a battering ram—ready for action.

"Down, boy," he whispered, trying as best he could to adjust himself. At least enough so that he could gather his things for his shower.

He inhaled and exhaled a few times and concentrated deeply, willing himself to go down. After a few agonizing minutes, his erection lay semiflaccid against his thigh. Throwing the duvet back, he went to get his case.

Jarred quickly showered, dressed in a pair of sweats

and a pullover, brushed his teeth and slipped his feet into his leather loafers. He walked into the kitchen, where Nevea was waiting with a cup of steaming hot coffee in hand.

"You will have to add sugar and milk if you like. I didn't know how you take it," she said shyly.

"I thought you didn't know how to cook," he said, taking the cup from her hands. Their fingers touched, and she jumped back, almost causing him to spill some of the hot liquid. "Careful," he murmured.

"Sorry," she said. "Making coffee is not cooking. I just measure the grinds and pour in water."

"True. However, it still takes skill." Jarred put milk and sugar in his cup and sipped. "This is good."

"Thank you," she said happily. "We can order breakfast and pick it up if you want."

"No need. I bought the fixings for breakfast last night when I went out." He stepped around the island, grabbed what he needed from the fridge and began to make French toast, bacon and eggs.

"Who taught you to cook?" Nevealise asked.

"My mom made sure all of us knew how to cook. She wanted us to know how to be independent and fend for ourselves. So she taught us. I have to say, it's a much-appreciated lesson. It comes in handy." He grinned, handing her a plate. "Eat and be merry."

"Want to hear something funny?" she asked, cutting into her French toast.

"What?"

"My mom taught my brothers how to cook, but not me." She laughed softly.

"Huh?" he questioned. A frown furrowed his brow.

"Cedric and Elijah hated it, too. See, my mom's way

of thinking was that Daddy always wanted a home-cooked meal, but he had a problem with men cooking, even though some of the greatest chefs in the world are men. In my father's mind the household duties were 'women's work.' It was so bad we only had takeout when he was away on business trips. I mean, can you imagine being ill with children, but still having to make a home-cooked meal? And let's not talk about the times he'd call her an hour or two before coming home to tell her that he was bringing some business associates for dinner." Nevealise snorted in disgust. "She found herself cooking and cleaning all the time. As we got older, my brothers did a lot of the cooking. My father had no idea that some of those meals he was eating were cooked by his sons."

"Did your mother ever tell him that it was too much for her?" Jarred asked quietly.

"I used to hear little bits and pieces when I was younger. Not enough to say that she was totally against being a housewife when we were little. As we got older, I know she wanted a career. She has a degree. As a matter of fact she has three. My dad just refused to let her work."

Jarred remained quiet, letting Nevea tell her story. He had a feeling she hadn't told it in a long time, if ever.

"Early childhood education and mathematics are her specialties. She wanted to teach kids with learning disabilities. She would tutor some of the neighborhood kids, but somehow, Josiah found a way to ruin that, as well," Nev said angrily, stabbing at her eggs. "So she spent her days helping us with our homework and tutoring us. We all excelled in our studies thanks to her."

"What did she do when you all went off to college?"

"There's a six- and seven-year age gap between me and my brothers. When they went off to college, I became the hostess alongside my mother. Only I was clumsy, and couldn't cook. I felt bad. The one time I tried to help out in the kitchen I dang near burned the house down." She snickered.

Jarred winced. Ooh, he could only imagine how that turned out.

"What did your father do?" he asked.

"Other than having the kitchen remodeled, my father didn't say or do anything. He never knew that I was the one who caused the fire. However, my mother lit into me. She was livid. After that I was banned from all things kitchen related. So I read a lot, joined the computer and math clubs at school, and that was the start of my journey. Besides her normal routine, Mom did a lot of charity work. Mostly for her church. But she never did get a career."

"I'm sorry," he said quietly. Her parents had always seemed happy to him. Her mother, Clara, was so regal. A beautiful woman just like her daughter.

"Why? You didn't do anything. You know, the one thing that I couldn't understand was how my father became such good friends with yours. I mean, your father always seemed so loving to his wife. Kat and I used to catch them sneaking a kiss all the time," Nev said, lowering her lashes.

"Yeah, they're still doing that."

"I would watch what your parents would do and run home and tell my mom. I mean, your dad worked late hours, but still had time for his family. He still expressed how much he loved and respected you all. I admired that quality in him."

"Thank you. I'll be sure to tell him the next time I talk to him." Listening to Nevea speak so highly of his father made Jarred feel ashamed of himself. Here he was, complaining about the mess his dad had left him and his brothers. He never realized how lucky he was to have him, how much it must have cost both his parents to give them a comfortable lifestyle. His dad had surpassed "comfortable" a long time ago, as had Josiah Tempest.

"Sometimes trying to stay on top makes people hard-hearted. I guess in some instances you have to be in order to keep people from taking advantage of you," Jarred said softly.

"That's not true and you know it. People tell me all the time how savvy a businessman my father is. How much they learned from him. Yet he taught strangers, helped strangers, before he did his own children. Does that sound like a great businessman to you?"

Considering the state Tempest Mortgage was in, Jarred wasn't about to comment on that subject. He recalled a lesson his father once taught him: Never kick a man when he's down, because you never knew where you'd be one day. That person you mocked might just be the one to save you. Jarred took those words to heart.

Nevertheless, he needed to have a conversation with his father. There was something to this whole Tempest Mortgage thing. He was sure of it. William Manning didn't make his millions by making stupid business moves. There had to be a method to the man's madness.

"Nevea, you do know you can be great at one thing and lousy at another, right? Your dad may have been a bad husband and father, but can you truly say that he wasn't a great businessman? Before you answer, think about it. You all lived in a mansion, on only your father's income."

"Of course we lived well. My father is a master at manipulation."

"Manipulation is a part of business. You should know this, since you own a business yourself. A business that appears to be thriving. So you had to have learned something from your father." Jarred knew he was reaching, but he just needed her to let go of some of her anger. He didn't like to see her unhappy.

"No, I didn't. Your brother taught me what I needed to know about business."

Jarred was taken aback. "My brother?"

"Yes, Brice. Brice dated my best friend in college. We've been close ever since. I'm surprised you didn't know this. Brice and Jasmine were hot and heavy in school. Anyway, when I decided I wanted to open my own lounge, Brice helped me from start to finish. I didn't have enough money at the time to build the way I wanted, so your brother stepped in and became my silent partner."

Jarred knew his mouth was hanging open. He didn't know what to say. Brice?

"That's why he has the reserved table," Jarred said in a hushed tone.

"Exactly."

"He never said a word," Jarred whispered. Apparently, there was more to his brother than he thought.

"Why would he? I tried to pay him back, but he wouldn't take it. So the next best thing was to make him a silent partner. You know he's superintelligent."

"Yes, I do. We've always known of Brice's intelligence. Enough talk about my brother. What are we doing today?" he asked, quickly changing the subject.

"I don't have a clue. I'll probably just rest up for tomorrow night."

"What's tomorrow night?"

"The lounge, remember?"

"Oh yes. I forgot. I guess you're performing tomorrow?" Jarred was going to make sure he was there.

"I may. Or I might just sit and enjoy everyone else."

"I don't think your fans will appreciate your being in the audience and not performing," he said.

"I am not a celebrity. I don't have fans. People come to Heavens to be entertained, and that's what they get—live entertainment. Whether it's me or someone else. A good show is what folks are looking for. I love sitting with the people, connecting with them. Keeps me grounded."

"Understandable. By the way, where'd you learn to sing like that?"

"I haven't the slightest idea. I just opened my mouth and started singing one day. I took dance classes, but not voice lessons."

"You had to have an inkling that you could sing. I mean, who doesn't pretend to sing when they're little?"

"Not me. I was into books," she said. "I still am. The club is like therapy to me. I chose the New Jersey location as a getaway from my normal surroundings. The added bonus is that I simply fell in love with the building and its surroundings."

"I know. You used to bombard us with some fact or another. Most of the time it was something you'd discovered in a book," Jarred mocked.

"Langston and Brice listened to me, or at least they

led me to believe that they did. You, however, never did. You used to tease me about reading so much."

"And look at me now. An attorney. Now I'm the one reading all the time. That's life. You never know what you're going to get.".

"That's right, you are a lawyer. I remember Brice bragging about you passing the New York, New Jersey and Connecticut bar exams. Good for you. I'd forgotten about that. I knew all of you except for Kat held positions in your father's company. However, you being an attorney totally slipped my mind."

The next thing he knew Nevea was out of her seat and flinging herself at him. "Congratulations! I am so proud of you," she cried, wrapping her arms around his neck.

His own arms instinctively enveloped her. If he knew telling her he was an attorney would elicit this kind of reaction from her, he'd have shared that bit of knowledge long before now. He held her close to him. Ah, man, he was in trouble. His body reacted to hers instantly. She must have realized what she'd done because she tried to move back. Too late. He was not releasing her.

"Don't go," he whispered, breathing in her flowery scent.

"Jarred?" she said softly.

"I want you, Nevea, and you want me, too," he murmured.

Chapter 9

Nevealise found herself backed up against the marble-topped kitchen island. Any objections she may have had were thwarted by Jarred's full lips sweeping down on hers. Of their own accord her arms tightened around him. Her body relaxed against his as she kissed him with the same intensity as he kissed her. Their tongues met and dueled together in a dance as old as time, as they took their fill of one another, neither relenting their hold.

Now this is a kiss. All the books she'd read on kissing were paying off in a big way. But she had a feeling there was more that Jarred was going to teach her before this was over.

As if he'd read her mind, Jarred tilted her head to the side, deepening the kiss. His hands slid down her spine to her backside, where he grasped her butt, pulling her close.

Nevealise gasped into his mouth at the feel of his erection rubbing against her. Her little experiment with Chauncey in college was nothing compared to Jarred's maleness. Releasing her hips, he glided his hand up under her shirt to cup her breast. She tore her lips from his and dropped her head back, crying out, "Oh my!" Thrusting her chest forward, she held on to the countertop, allowing him better access.

She was on fire. Her breath came in spurts, hot and shallow. Not wasting any time, he swiftly lifted her T over her head and tossed it to the floor. Pushing her bra down, Jarred bent and tasted her breasts. Nevealise moaned as his tongue did wicked things to her nipples.

"Jarred," she panted.

"I know, baby. Enjoy," he whispered against a puckered peak.

Nevealise gripped the island tighter and Jarred had his way with her breasts, alternating from one to the other.

Her hands left the countertop to take hold of his head and pull him closer. She really didn't know what she was doing; she simply knew what she liked and acted on instinct.

She cried out in dismay when his wet mouth finally left her breast. "Wh-what?"

"A bed. We need a bed, Nevea," he murmured.

Taking her by the hand, he walked her to her bedroom, where he gently pushed her back onto the bed.

She watched between lowered lashes as he began to undress. Taking off his shirt first, he tossed it onto a nearby chair. His hand went to the band of his sweatpants and her entire body stiffened. He must have noticed, because he halted his movements. Instead of removing his pants, he sat on the bed next to her, giving her a questioning stare.

"Nevea, have you…have you ever been with a man before?"

"Yes." She wouldn't tell him that the man had been a twenty-year-old college student—and she had been nineteen. It had been the first time for them both. "Why?"

"I was just wondering," he said, still gazing down at her. Her reaction had him wondering if she'd ever had sex before. No doubt his mind told him that there was no way she hadn't been with a man, not at twenty-eight years old. But her actions had probably told him that she was inexperienced.

"I know how this works, Jarred," she said, to convince him.

"Say what?"

"I've been with a man before. If you don't want to—"

"Bite your tongue. Of course I want to," he growled, leaning down to capture her lips. Nevealise latched on to his tongue as if it were her lifeline.

She felt her bra being unhooked, and the confining material falling from her body and onto the bed.

Releasing her lips, he ran his tongue diagonally over her nipples and then slowly traveled down across her abdomen.

Nevealise held her breath as she felt his hot, moist mouth on her belly button. Her vaginal muscles tightened under his ministrations, and he hadn't touched that part of her yet. The mere thought of him kissing and touching her there aroused her senses. The feelings he evoked in her were so foreign she didn't think she could handle them. Nothing she'd read about had prepared her for what Jarred was doing to her.

His hands roamed over her breasts, causing a hot, molten sensation to course through her. Nevealise couldn't stop herself. Feeling like a fiery inferno, she began squirming around on the bed, trying to release whatever it was that had hold of her. Something was happening to her. She didn't have any idea what it was, but she needed to release it. If only she knew how... Her research had talked about orgasms, but what she was feeling now was indescribable.

His hand traveled under her shorts and her panties to reach that part of her that craved his touch. When he inserted one finger inside her Nevealise almost came off the bed, she bucked so hard.

"Jarred," she cried.

"It's okay, sweetheart. I have you. Just go with the flow," he whispered, continuing to bring her pleasure with his masterful finger.

She tossed her head back and forth. She took hold of the duvet and held on tight.

"Nevea, relax. Lie back and enjoy," he murmured, his voice husky with passion.

"Oh, goodness!" she cried, as she felt his finger moving in and out of her. Her toes tingled; sweat covered her brow; her body jerked and spasmed, out of control. Nev's spine bent like a bow as she felt a warm liquid trickle out of her.

And then his hands left her and she felt bereft. She felt her shorts and underwear being removed, but she couldn't move. It was as if she were under some kind of spell...an out-of-body experience that she'd read about. Surely the sounds emitting from her lips were not from her. This had to be someone else begging Jarred to take her.

Her eyes flew open and she saw him move away from her and get off the bed. Maybe she should have kept them closed, because now she saw him in all his naked glory, standing there. Her gaze widened when she saw the erection protruding from between his legs as if it were standing at attention. Her own legs clenched together at the sight of him. There was no way he was going to fit inside her.

"What's wrong, sweetheart?"

She quivered. "Uh, Jarred, I don't think you're going to fit," she breathed.

"Trust me. I will," he assured her.

"No. I don't think so. Chauncey wasn't that big and it hurt," she said in a horrified voice.

"Who the hell is Chauncey?" he demanded.

"Chauncey was the guy I had sex with before," she responded, still staring at Jarred's erection. Despite his assurances, she feared he'd tear up her insides when he entered her.

"Nevea, just how many sexual partners have you had?" he asked softly.

"I already told you. Chauncey. We were in college," she said in a voice that quivered.

"One person or one time?" he asked with a quirk of his brow.

"One person and one time."

"Ah… I see. Well, evidently this Chaney dude didn't know what he was doing—"

"Not Chaney. *Chauncey*," she insisted.

"Whatever. Trust me, he didn't know how to please a woman. I won't hurt you. It may be a little uncomfortable at first, but it gets better, and I can guarantee I'll bring you more pleasure than you could ever dream of. That's a promise," he soothed, coming to sit on the bed next to her and pulling her into his arms. He turned her face to his. "Trust me," he said again, before placing his lips on hers. He kissed her thoroughly, while simultaneously playing with her nipple.

Before she knew it, her fears subsided, replaced by desire. In seconds she was writhing on the bed. Jarred pushed her back and lay on top of her, using his knee to spread her legs wide. He settled himself at the V of her thighs, and she felt him at her center and flinched.

"Uh-uh, no tensing. Relax. If you tighten up it will hurt," he whispered against her lips.

"I don't know, Jarred," she said, hearing the panic return to her voice. How could she fear something so much and want it so badly at the same time?

"Give me your hand," he urged.

Trusting him, she did so.

"You will be in control," he said, bringing her palm to his erection. He pressed it over him, letting her get a feel of him. "Now you guide me in."

"How?"

Jarred showed her what he was talking about by covering her hand with his own and guiding himself to her center. He covered her mouth with his and deftly surged up and into her. Nevealise caught her breath and then released it.

"Are you okay?" he groaned.

She nodded.

"Good. See, I told you," he said, and began to move within her.

Nevealise felt full. He filled every inch of her, but in a good way.

"Move with me, sweetheart," she heard him say.

She did as he asked, lifting her hips to take in every inch of him and pulling back as he eased slightly out of her. Repeatedly she mimicked his motions, until she felt those same sensations as before. Oh goodness, it was happening again. The inferno was building inside her, demanding release.

"Jarred," she moaned.

"Good. Don't hold back, Nevea. Just go with it," he growled. He continued pumping in and out of her, faster than before.

She could only whimper beneath him, unable to utter actual words.

"Let go, Nevea! Come for me now!" he bellowed.

And just like that she let go. She quaked and trembled uncontrollably. She wailed as her body felt as if it had exploded into a million little pieces.

"Oh my!" she shouted.

Jarred bucked on top of her, faster and faster, until she felt his hot liquid enter her. When he came, she went off again. What was wrong with her? She couldn't stop the sensations that hit her. She was out of control.

He lowered himself to her, his breath coming hard and fast in a rhythm that matched her own.

"You did great, sweetheart," he said moments later, in a strangled voice.

Nevealise breathed in and out, trying to suck air into her lungs. Her body still trembled from the things Jarred had done to it.

"I told you we'd fit," he said, finally dislodging himself. Something inside her cried out for him to remain

Chapter 10

Nevealise twirled around in her dress. She looked at herself from all angles in the mirror of her dressing room. She'd chosen the short, sequined number on the spur of the moment, having arrived at the lounge late, with only moments to rummage through her gowns.

Jarred was the cause of her tardiness. He'd kept her in bed most of the day. They'd left the house only for a stroll around the city. They'd walked for hours, taking in the sights, and Nevealise had felt like a new person. A woman reborn. He'd done things to her body that she didn't think were possible. And she couldn't wait to return the favor.

She turned around again, trying to get a better view of the dress in the mirror. Nevealise had purchased it a year ago with her friends Jasmine and Dominica. It had been Jasmine's idea that they perform a number as the Supremes for some fund-raising event of hers.

Nevealise and Dominica had protested all the way to the stage. However, the number they did had been a success. Now here she was again, in the same dress she'd protested against.

"Just what are you trying to prove, Nev?" she asked her reflection. But she didn't answer herself. Instead, she began to apply her makeup.

Thank goodness for Jasmine's expertise in the makeup department. She'd taught Nevealise how to use it to highlight her natural looks. Wearing makeup wasn't an everyday occurrence for her. She wore it only when she sang at Heavens and for special occasions. She applied the finishing touches, gave herself another once-over and prepared to go out onstage.

The MC began to speak. That was her cue that it was almost time. She placed her hand on her stomach to quell the butterflies suddenly having a party in there. Normally she wasn't nervous when she went onstage, but tonight Jarred was out in the audience. She was having such a hard time breathing, she hoped she could get through her numbers, especially the first one, a soulful, sexy song.

The MC called her name and the audience's applause reached her ears.

That's my cue. Nevealise dragged in a deep breath and stepped out of her dressing room.

She took center stage, waited for the spotlight to catch her and began to sing Joss Stone's "Lady." Nevealise could identify with every lyric and moved her body accordingly, giving the audience a good show. She finished the number to the thunderous clapping of the crowd and moved directly into another song. This one was true to her heart—Aretha Franklin's "(You

Make Me Feel) Like a Natural Woman." Nevealise gave it everything she had in her. The band was on point, following her lead and not missing a single beat. She acknowledged them, and when she turned back, her eyes lit on Jarred. He was sitting at a table in the front. His eyes met and held hers, and despite the crowded lounge it was as if they were the only two people in the room. Somehow she continued with the song, pouring out her heart with each emotionally inspired lyric. Far off she could hear people singing along with her. One was shouting, "You're bringing the house down, Nev." But she ignored the voices and kept her eyes on the man who'd inspired her to sing it. Her pulse quickened as she got further into her number. Her arousal was at a fever pitch. She could feel the moistening of her panties. She was almost relieved when the song came to an end, fearing she might fall to pieces right there onstage.

She tore her eyes away from Jarred and took several deep breaths before looking out into the crowd. Some had made their way to the stage. The aisles were packed, with people standing, cheering and catcalling.

Her heart was singing. *Wow!* They really liked it. She hadn't sung with that much heart and soul in a long time. If ever.

People were still applauding and filling the aisles.

"Thank you! Thank you!" she said, taking a bow.

Nevealise streamlined her gaze to focus in on Jarred. He gave her two thumbs-up, and then was whistling and applauding along with the others. He blew a kiss at her, causing her smile to widen. She began to laugh heartily, lifted her hand to the crowd, waved, and then turned and left the stage.

* * *

"Wow!" Jarred exclaimed. That was awesome. He looked around Heavens, at the people still standing and applauding. Nevea had received a standing ovation. It was well deserved. She sang the hell out of that song. The queen herself, Aretha, would have been proud of her. At first when she'd begun singing he'd smirked. He knew she was messing with him. But when she started singing "(You Make Me Feel) Like a Natural Woman" it had struck a chord with him.

And damn. That little piece of a dress she wore clung to her every curve. When she'd first stepped into view he'd almost come out of his chair. A flash of arousal had sent a signal from his brain to his lower region. His zipper had tightened against him. Her hair was pinned back from her face in a bun at the nape of her neck, and the red lipstick she wore added to her sexiness. Nevea was beautiful and she was his. All his.

Warmth radiated throughout his body. So much so that his insides felt as if they were vibrating. His face gleamed as he bobbed his head up and down, and bounced from one foot to the other, not able to contain his excitement. "Wow!" he said again. He couldn't get what had just happened out of his head. He was proud of her.

"You're one lucky man," some guy standing next to his table was saying.

"Word," another said.

"That sista' didn't sing. She sa-a-ang that! Somebody needs to give her a record deal," yet another declared.

Jarred could only smile. He knew he was showing all thirty-two of his teeth, his smile was so broad.

"Yes, yes, I am lucky," he said.

There was a tap on his shoulder. He turned to see Norman standing next to him.

"You want to go to the back where she's at?" he asked.

"Sure," Jarred promptly replied. He followed Norman to Nevea's dressing room.

"You can go on in. I'm positive she wouldn't mind." Norman smirked.

Jarred flashed him a smile. "Thanks, man," he said, and then turned the knob.

Nevea turned to face him just as soon as the door opened, a glass of wine in her hand. She'd told him that she always took a few sips of wine after her performances. He'd told her that she did it backward. Most people would have a drink before a performance. Jarred liked her quirky ways. They turned him on, but then again, everything about her turned him on.

"Did you enjoy the performance?" she asked.

Without saying a word, he advanced toward her, took the glass out of her hand and lowered his lips to hers. Her arms wrapped around him as he pulled her into his embrace. Her body relaxed against his as she returned his kiss with the same pent-up passion that he felt for her. Their tongues met and danced, neither relenting, both fighting for dominance. He tilted her head, deepening the kiss. He could taste the wine on her tongue. He pulled back, only to drag in a breath and capture her lips again. His hands left her head and roamed across her hips, pulling her closer and rubbing her against his erection as he captured her cries in his mouth.

Backing her up against her vanity, he pushed his

hand up under her dress—and paused. She wasn't wearing underwear.

"Bad girl," he growled against her lips, and then pushed her legs apart and inserted a finger inside her.

She moaned, and waved her hands as if she didn't know what to do next. She was a novice at lovemaking, but every move she made only caused him to want her more, need her more. He removed his finger and pulled her dress up to her waist, pushed his zipper down and then drew a condom from his pocket.

"Put it on me, Nevea," he said, handing the condom to her. With nervous fingers she sheathed him. "Hold on," he demanded. In seconds he aligned himself with her center and pushed inside her. She was wet and ready for him.

"Damn," he whispered, continuing to plunge in and ease out of her, faster and harder each time. He was pumping like a man possessed. She was holding on to his shoulders, her face buried in the crook of his neck, making little passionate noises. He felt her muscles tighten around him. On the peak of an orgasm, he pulled out almost all the way and then thrust into her, deep and hard, sending her over the edge. She screamed her release against his neck. His own release followed seconds after.

Jarred laid his head against hers, unable to stop the erratic beating of his heart or catch his breath.

"Whoo," he gasped. "That was…that was unbelievable."

"Yes," she choked out. "It was."

She was still trembling against him. They stood there wrapped in each other's arms. He couldn't move.

He didn't want to move. He was still hard inside her. He gulped and kissed her firmly on the lips.

"Baby, I think I have an addiction," he said, still winded.

"Really?" she said, panting. "And what would that be?"

"You," he growled, and began to move inside her again.

She gasped and then began to move with him. "I concur."

It was another hour before they left Heavens and drove back to Nevea's, where their lovemaking continued.

Chapter 11

Jarred sat facing the picture window in his office, thinking about his time with Nevea the last few days. He'd turned off all forms of communication, not wanting anyone to intrude on their time together. His decision to drive out to her town house had been bold, spontaneous and worth every mile he'd traveled. They'd made love hard and often in almost every room in Nevea's home. He'd hated to leave her and her bed.

He swung his chair around as the door to his office opened, and groaned inwardly. He'd gotten a call from both Langston and Brice, wanting to know his whereabouts. He'd forgotten that he'd told Langston he would see him in the morning. Not wanting to invade Nevealise's privacy, he hadn't said anything to his brothers about being with her.

"So the prodigal son has returned," Langston said, as he and Brice walked into his office.

"Don't you two believe in knocking?" he grumbled. It was bad enough he had to be here instead of with Nevea, but these two brought him back to the realization that playtime was over. He had a lot of work to do.

"Yes, but because we haven't seen you since Thursday we figured you owed us," Langston said.

"If you say so. Have we gotten anywhere with our computer problem?"

"No, but I thought of something that no one else seemed to have," Brice said.

"And that would be?" Jarred asked.

"We get Nev in here to break into the computers."

Jarred stiffened. He'd never thought to ask for Nevea's help. Considering how she felt about her father and anything connected to his name, Jarred doubted very seriously that she would help. However, Brice was correct. If anyone could do it, Nevea could.

"She'd never go for it," Jarred said quietly.

"Why not?" Langston asked.

"Her father is not one of her favorite people." Brice cut in before Jarred could respond.

"I kind of figured that from the night at Heavens," Langston said.

Jarred listened to both of them going back and forth. He would broach the subject with her. Making love to Nevea had been glorious, and to find out that he was her first real lover was a bonus. There was that Chaney person, but he didn't count.

After they'd made love the first time, both Jarred and Nevea had fallen asleep. Once they awakened he had run a bath and they'd both soaked in it. He'd mainly run it for her.

Jarred had also realized his mistake: he hadn't used

a condom. So he ran out to the store and picked up a box. It was sort of like shutting the barn door after the horse left, but better late than never. He truly hadn't intended to make love to her without a condom. It just happened. Jarred didn't regret making love to her, only that he hadn't protected her.

They'd left her apartment and he'd hung out with her at Heavens on Saturday. It was then that he realized the club was truly a special place for her. She was sultry, bold and sure of herself when she was singing.

He'd left Nevea's place early Sunday morning. She'd had to prepare for a series of meetings on Monday. He hadn't wanted to keep her from her work, so he'd gone home. He'd spent yesterday watching movies and thinking about Nevea. He'd made himself unavailable to everyone but her. He'd spoken to her several times, but it wasn't the same as seeing her.

"Jarred, are you listening to anything we've said?" he heard Langston asking.

"What?"

"He's in his own little world, apparently," Brice said drily.

"I guess so," Langston agreed. "What's wrong with you lately, bro? You haven't heard from crazy Lainey, have you?"

"What are you going on about, Langston? And why would Lainey be contacting me? I haven't seen her since she left," Jarred barked.

"Don't bite my head off. You've been acting strange. Missing work. Not answering your phone. What was I supposed to think?"

"Anything but Lainey. I wouldn't give her the time of day," Jarred snapped.

"So you're finally over her?" Brice asked quietly.

"Yes, I am. I have no interest in Lainey Gaines. No interest at all."

"Well, that's good to hear," Langston said. "So where have you been?"

"Out."

"Come on, Jarred. I know it's a woman, so you may as well confess. You've been preoccupied and smiling a lot. I know you can't be smiling about anything going on here lately, so the only other logical conclusion would be a woman. So who is she?"

"Why are you so interested in my personal life?"

"Because I'm your brother." He shrugged.

Jarred burst out laughing. "Being my brother gives you the right to know my every move?"

"Yes. It's written somewhere."

"Where?" both Jarred and Brice asked at the same time.

"I don't know. It just is."

"You may as well tell him that you've been spending your days and nights with Nev," Brice stated.

"No-o-o," Langston said, his head bouncing back and forth between the two of them. Then he stared at Jarred in surprise.

Jarred was glaring at Brice. His little brother talked too much.

"Just how do you know this, Brice?"

"I knew you were really interested in her at the club. Your reaction to her was strong. Also, the day you got that call I knew it was Nev. You'd been trying to reach her and she wasn't returning your calls." He shrugged. "Simple deduction."

"For real, you have a thing going on with Nev?" Langston asked.

"Yes," Jarred admitted. "We've been seeing each other. It's hard because of our jobs. She travels all over the world for hers. I just don't know how it's going to work, with her out of town so much." He sighed.

"What exactly is it that she does?" Langston asked.

"She's a consultant for the government, and she's working on designing a video game. It's an educational game. Nevea has so many jobs I can't keep up with them. Hell, I can barely keep up with the one *I* have."

"I thought Heavens was her job," Langston said, sounding confused.

"No, she owns Heavens along with her silent partner, our brother over there," Jarred said matter-of-factly.

"Brice, you're part owner in Heavens?" Langston questioned, looking confused.

"Boy, you two seem to have covered a lot of ground in a very little time," Brice said sarcastically.

"It's been three weeks," Jarred answered.

"It sounds serious," Langston said.

Jarred shrugged. "Maybe. Maybe not. It's too early to tell."

"I call bullshit," Brice snickered. "Who do you think you're fooling, Jarred? You've been with her every chance you can get. Since we've been sitting here you've looked down at your watch three times. You're waiting on her call. Nah, bro, it's serious. You're just too afraid to admit it."

"Not on my part, Brice. Hers. I don't know if she's looking for or is ready for anything serious. She has some real issues with her father, ones that in my opinion border on the unhealthy side. Josiah, from what I've heard, controlled everything her mother did. Nevea resents that and him."

"If he was smart he would have brought her on board. Maybe his company wouldn't be in so much trouble," Langston said.

Brice spoke up then. "Nev has every right to feel the way she does about her father. He used her."

Jarred's eyes swung to him. The lines on his brother's face were taut, like he was trying to control his anger.

"Used her how?" Jarred asked.

"This doesn't leave this room. Jarred, you have to assure me that you won't let Nev know I told you," Brice said.

Jarred didn't say anything. Depending on what it was, he wasn't sure he could make a promise like that.

"Jarred, Nev will tell you herself soon enough. I just want you to understand why she feels the way she does. I can tell you have strong feelings for her. Just give her space to let her open up about it. That's all I ask," Brice said, throwing up his hands.

"Okay," Jarred agreed reluctantly.

"Nev designed the software and hardware on Tempest's computers. Josiah had her design and install a special spyware and computer program with the promise of bringing her on board in an upper-management position. She did what he asked and he reneged on the deal. Nev still hasn't forgiven him. He paid for her brothers' schooling but not hers. Fortunately for her, she's so intelligent she didn't have to pay out of pocket for anything. What her scholarships didn't cover her brothers did. As wealthy as her father is, he wouldn't bring her into the company, nor would he help finance her business."

"That's why she calls him a master manipulator," Jarred whispered. "Damn, if he wasn't older than our father, I'd kick his chauvinistic behind myself. What a douche."

"Why would Dad want to get involved with a man like Josiah Tempest?" Langston mused, a scowl on his face.

"He had his reasons. Dad's not stupid. He knows what he's doing. I just wish he'd fill us in on it," Brice said.

"I hope so. It's taking everything in me not to call the egomaniac out," Jarred snarled. "Nevea's his daughter, but he basically made her fend for herself because she wouldn't bend to his will. Who the hell does that to their child? Do you know how many crazy people there are out there waiting to take advantage of a young, vulnerable girl? Not to mention she's simply beautiful."

"She is. Inside and out," Brice said.

"Do you know she doesn't know how to cook?" Jarred said.

"So?" both brothers said.

"Hire a cook for her," Langston snapped.

"That's not what I mean, you two. I mean her mother didn't teach her, because she didn't want her to be a slave to any man. Also, Nevea doesn't take care of herself. She goes days without eating and lives on energy drinks. She has a fridge full of those drinks and no food worth eating. I've been texting her to remind her to eat. I also cook for her when she's with me. I make sure she has at least three meals a day," he said fervently.

"Sounds like a man in love to me. What do you think, Brice?" Langston's smile was wide.

"For sure," Brice said, giving Langston a high five.

"I am not," Jarred grumbled, glancing again at his watch.

"Why don't you just call her?" Langston said. "It's the only way you're going to stop looking down at your wristwatch and get some work done."

"How's Emerson working out in his new position?" Jarred asked, trying his best to ignore that last statement.

"He loves it. Since he's practically doing the same thing he was before, I can't see why he wouldn't like it," Langston said.

"Good," Jarred replied. "It's not the same job, really. Now he's in charge. Has he gotten anywhere with the security team?"

"Not yet. I've been working with him mostly," Brice said.

"I say we continue to work on this thing with Tempest, but at the same time continue on with our other work. We can't get so involved with Tempest that we neglect Manning Enterprises," Jarred said.

"I couldn't agree more," Brice said. "You and Langston concentrate on Manning's, and I'll work on figuring out the problem with Tempest. Emerson and I have everything under control. But, Jarred, we may need Nev. We'll use her as a last resort."

"That's if she agrees. I have a feeling she won't," Jarred said.

"Maybe not, but we'll have to try if it comes to that." Brice shrugged.

"Well, now that I know you're okay, I'll go back to my office and get some work done," Langston said, tongue in cheek.

"I'm out of here, too," Brice said, standing up and walking to the door. Langston was right on his heels.

"I'll talk to you two before I leave for the night," Jarred said.

Langston and Brice walked out of his office, shutting the door behind them.

Jarred decided to put a call in to Human Resources. He needed a secretary, since his seemed to have gone missing. At least a temp for now. He'd go with a temp to see how the person worked out before hiring anyone.

Jarred picked up his desk phone and dialed.

"Hi, Mr. Manning."

"Hi, Martha. Can you see about getting me a temp for a couple of weeks?"

"Sure, Mr. Manning. I'll get right on it."

"Thank you."

"You're welcome. Bye, Mr. Manning."

Jarred put his receiver down, picked up a folder on his desk and got to work.

Chapter 12

Exhausted and aching, Nevealise could barely concentrate on what she was doing. She and Jarred had had a sex-a-thon of sorts over the weekend. She was sore in places she'd never known existed. After Jarred had left her yesterday morning, she'd again soaked in a hot tub. Her weekend with Jarred had been a great one. They'd had fun together. She loved watching him cook and he loved cooking for her. They had laughed, talked, made love and done it all again, especially the making love part.

Nevealise had to admit that for the first time in a long while, she was happy, and it wasn't work related.

"It looks like you have to read some more books, Nev, if you're going to keep up with Jarred," she whispered to herself. "Or at least be in the same league." She felt inadequate in a way. As if he were doing all the

work. She wanted to learn how to give him the pleasure he'd given her. He kept telling her she was doing
fine, and she believed him. However, she wanted to
be secure enough to take charge herself. To start their
lovemaking rather than wait for him to start. To lead
the way.

But she couldn't do her research right now. It was
time to get back to work. She had a meeting in a few
minutes. The second of a scheduled three. Suddenly,
she didn't feel like being here. For the first time she
had a life, and she wanted to enjoy every minute of it.

The shrill sound of her cell phone ringing brought
Nevealise out of her reverie. After reaching for it and
looking at the caller ID, she quickly answered.

"Jarred, hello! This is a surprise," she said cheer-
fully.

"Wow, someone is chipper this morning. I wonder
why that is?" Nevealise could hear his laughter through
the receiver. "Could it be that someone got some good
lovin' put on her?"

Nevealise blushed from the crown of her head to
the soles of her feet.

"What? Nothing to say, my sexy songstress?"

Oh my word. He was never going to let her forget
that song she'd sung for him, nor their makeout ses-
sion afterward.

"How are you feeling this morning?" she heard
Jarred say in his jubilant voice, not giving her time to
answer his first question.

"I'm so sore I can barely walk," she blurted out.

There was a pause on the other end of the phone.
Nevealise wondered if she had spoken too soon. She
didn't want him to think that she hadn't enjoyed their

romp—that was far from the truth. She had enjoyed it a little too much.

"Sore in a good way," she quickly added.

She heard a sigh of what sounded like relief from the other end, and then Jarred's boisterous laughter. "Good as in I did the damn thing?" His concern was now replaced with cockiness.

Nevealise covered her face with her hand and whimpered. It was good he wasn't sitting in front of her to see her reddened skin. She was sure she was flushed from top to bottom.

"You are so conceited it's ridiculous," she grumbled. "Not only can't I walk properly, I can't concentrate on what I'm doing. My face has been so flushed, and from the permanent smile on it, everyone knows what I was doing over the weekend."

Nevealise knew that was the case, because in her first meeting she'd been teasingly called out on it by one of her team members. "Nev's got a man!" her co-worker had said. Nevealise didn't have to respond; the blush on her face said it all.

Jarred chuckled harder. "Stop laughing!" Nevealise exclaimed and then started to chuckle herself.

"I'm sorry, sweetheart. Admit it. Facts are facts. You were singing in the church choir a few times. And that soprano note you hit was enough to drive me wild. I can't wait to do it again."

"I don't have time to play with you. I have a meeting in less than five minutes," she murmured.

"Confess. I gave it to you good. I want to hear you say it," he teased. Nevealise could hear the smile in his voice. The arrogant so-and-so. He was just too sure of himself. If truth be told, Jarred had touched parts of her body that she hadn't known could bring her pleasure, as well as release. She'd had too many orgasms to count. She'd gone from not having sex at all to not being able to go without it. Still, she wouldn't admit it.

"I will not," she said snootily.

"All kidding aside," he said. "I missed having you in my arms last night."

Nevealise smiled inwardly. She didn't think she could ever be this happy, but she was. "I missed being in your arms, too. I can't wait to see you this weekend, Jarred."

"Nor I you. No shop talk from either of us. Not one mention of bits, bytes, bugs and all that other computer jargon from you, and I won't harp about my constant headache of a job. It'll just be you, me and the sounds of some good lovemaking. You need to do whatever it takes to relieve your soreness, sexy girl, because I plan on keeping you on your back this weekend, as well," he mock threatened.

Nevealise was shocked. Her mouth hung open. "Oh, really?" she gulped.

"Yes. Count on it. I love the way you scream my name. *'Jarred... Jarred!'*" he mimicked.

Nevealise didn't think her face could get any redder. She did remember calling his name a few times. "You know a gentleman wouldn't repeat that."

"A gentleman wouldn't. Who says I'm a gentleman? Not in the bedroom, baby. Not in the bedroom. Besides, I like it when you scream my name. All of your inhibitions are left behind and the wanton goddess is released," he said with a chuckle.

Oh, goodness, Jarred was killing her. Her thighs clenched together tightly. In a move totally unlike her,

Nevealise responded, "Humph, don't be surprised if you're the one screaming *my* name."

"Oh, hurt me, baby. Hurt me."

Nevealise was spared from responding by a knock at her door. She quickly looked down at her watch and grimaced. She was late.

"Listen, Jarred, someone's at my door. I'm late for my meeting. I'll talk to you later tonight," she said quickly.

"I'll talk to you this evening, love."

"Gotta go. Bye," she said, disconnecting.

"Come in," she called out. Nevealise watched as one of the techs, Melissa, pushed the door open and walked into Nevealise's temporary office with a huge smile on her face.

"Hey, Nev," Melissa chirped. "I know you're on cloud nine from your 'secret' rendezvous, but you're late for our meeting."

"I know. I was just coming. I had an emergency call," Nevealise lied, and lowered her head so that Melissa wouldn't see her flushed face.

"Yeah, I get those emergency calls sometimes, too." She giggled.

Nevealise felt her cheeks heat even more. "On my way. Can you let them know? Give me a minute," she breathed.

"Sure thing. Wow, Nev's got a man. This is totally awesome!" Melissa said, and turned on her heels.

Quickly pulling herself together, Nevealise left her office. An hour later she was still in meetings. It looked as if she would be back and forth the rest of the week from Norfolk to Washington, and then on to Los Angeles. She heaved a disappointed sigh. *And there goes my week.*

Chapter 13

After Nevea called to let him know she wouldn't be available for the rest of the week, Jarred had been disappointed, but understood. Well, almost. She was working too hard. Flying from one place to another. When he'd finally gotten the chance to speak to her again, she'd been so tired he hadn't kept her on the phone long. Instead he told her to rest up and he'd see her over the weekend. But they'd missed their weekend because Nevea had been stuck in Los Angeles, and wouldn't be back in town until the following Wednesday. That's when Jarred had come up with a plan. His lady was tired and he was going to do something about it.

Jarred picked up the phone and dialed Brice's number.

"Brice, I need a favor," he said, then listened to his brother groan as if he were in pain.

"What now? Haven't you bogged me down with enough favors?" Brice griped.

"This has nothing to do with work," Jarred stated.

"What?" Brice's tone was a little less irritated and more questioning.

"I need you to set something up for me," Jarred said, and then went on to tell Brice his plans. He just hoped they worked. Knowing Nevea, she could be out in Timbuktu somewhere.

"Aren't I the youngest brother?" Brice snickered. "Why do I find myself constantly helping you out with your woman?"

"Shut the hell up, Brice. You're not constantly helping me out with Nevea. I just asked a favor. Are you going to do it or not?" Jarred snapped.

"You know I will. That's why you asked," Brice grumbled.

Jarred had a huge smile on his face. "Thanks, bro, and I promise to return the favor."

"Yeah, yeah, yeah. If I ever have to go through all of this to be with a woman, shoot me in the foot," he muttered.

Jarred knew that despite all Brice's "supposed" indignation, he would do anything to help him or Langston out. As they would do for him.

"I'll remind you of that one day." Jarred laughed.

"Whatever. Bye."

Jarred gave another boisterous laugh. Leave it to Brice to agree to help and then hang up on him.

He looked around his library and smiled. Little Miss Nevealise Tempest was in for a shock.

Nevealise sat at her reserved table in Heavens listening to the live band. There had already been someone who delivered the spoken word. The poem had been exquisite. She was now enjoying Rainbow, an up-and-coming band. The sound was good. Unique. A little bit of funk and blues.

This was the first time in two weeks that Nevealise had been able to relax. She'd been working nonstop. For some reason her work hadn't been as satisfying as it once was. The long hours were beginning to take their toll. Not only that, she hadn't seen Jarred at all in that time. Nevealise missed him something terrible. He'd called to say he wouldn't be able to see her until Sunday. She'd been disappointed, of course, but had understood, since she'd had to do the same thing to him.

Rainbow finished with a standing ovation. Nevealise was clapping hard for them, even though she hadn't heard the last of the song. She'd been too engrossed in her thoughts.

"Okay, ladies and gentlemen," called out the MC. "You all know that Heavens loves to showcase old as well as new talent. Tonight it's new talent. Let's hear it for—"

"Hey, Nev," Nevealise heard Brice say as he took a seat next to her. She looked around and saw Langston sitting next to him. Nevealise tried to discreetly look over their shoulders for Jarred. But he wasn't with them. She masked her disappointment with a smile, standing up she walked over to place a kiss on both Manning brothers' cheeks.

"You're not performing tonight?" Langston asked.

"Not that I know of. I'm just enjoying the show," she said, taking her seat.

"What the hell! What's Jarred doing?" Brice questioned, squinting his eyes.

Did he say Jarred? He couldn't have. Jarred was busy. Nevealise whipped her head around, but didn't spot him.

"I don't see Jarred. Where is he?" she asked anxiously. She hadn't realized until just now how much she missed him. She couldn't wait to see him.

"He's in front of us, onstage," Langston said, clearly perplexed.

Nevealise looked toward the stage, and sure enough, Jarred stood up there as if he hadn't a care in the world.

"What's he doing?" she asked quietly, her nerves becoming frayed now.

The lights dimmed and the next thing she knew Jarred was belting out a song, and not just any song. Robin Thicke's "Sex Therapy."

The song was so sexy, and everyone in the lounge knew he was singing it to her. He wasn't making it a secret. She was so embarrassed that she covered her face with her hands.

People were shouting and calling out all over the place.

"Honey, you are one lucky lady!" she heard a woman declare.

"Well, damn!" Brice exclaimed. "Go ahead, brother. Do the damn thing!"

"Brice, sit down," Langston said, laughing his head off. "He's singing that song, though. Haven't heard him sing in a long time. You knew about this, Brice?"

"Not at all. Well, I knew something, but not this," Brice said, applauding along with the crowd.

"I didn't know he could sing. He's never said anything," Nevealise stated shyly, remembering what she'd done for him weeks ago. To her utter chagrin, Jarred had the nerve to come get her from her seat and take her up onstage. He sang to her while at the same time swaying her in a slow dance. Both the song and the dance were decadent and sexy, and it was all for her. Her heart surged.

Jarred finished the song and kissed her right there in the middle of the stage. She was so into the kiss that she didn't hear all the catcalls. Her mind was on one person. The gorgeous man kissing her senseless.

"Missed you, baby," he whispered against her lips.

"I missed you, too," she whispered back.

"And that's how a Manning does it," Brice yelled in the background.

"Let's get out of here," Jarred muttered.

"Yes, let's," she agreed.

He released her, but held on to her hand, thanked the audience and led her back to her dressing room. Once inside, he closed and locked the door.

"Jarred, what the—?" she asked, when she found herself backed up against the door.

Whatever she was about to say stuck in her throat as his lips captured hers. Of their own accord, her arms came up around his neck. Her body relaxed into his as their kiss intensified. She gave as much as she got, and was enjoying every minute of it.

Jarred's hand reached up under her dress and in one fierce, possessive motion he ripped her underwear off. "Wrap your legs around me, Nevea," he demanded huskily.

Nevea pushed back against the door and did what he asked. Jarred freed himself from the confines of his trousers and boxers and pushed up into her.

"Oh, my," she cried softly.

"I need you, Nevea," he groaned.

"Yes," she murmured. "Yes."

"Shush," he said against her lips, continually surging into her. "Someone is standing just outside the door. You want them to hear us?"

That got her attention. "Oh, goodness, do you think they can hear us?" she asked on a ragged breath.

"No one's paying attention. Just try not to scream," he murmured.

He pushed up into her; she pushed down on him. They were both out of control. The only thing that could be heard in the dressing room was their loud breathing.

"Jarred, I'm about to come."

"Bite down on my shoulder," he demanded.

Her orgasm hit her hard. Just as it did, she did as he commanded, biting down so hard that Jarred would probably have a mark on his shoulder. He surged up into her one last time before releasing into her.

"Oh my! I guess that is what is referred to as a quickie," she said.

She felt him shaking against her. He was laughing at her.

"That, my beautiful Nevea, was definitely a quickie," he choked out. "Man, you're beautiful."

"Thank you. Now how are we going to get out of here without everyone knowing what we've been doing?"

"I hate to break it to you, sweetheart, but they knew what we'd be doing the minute I sang that song," he said, releasing her legs. After he adjusted her clothes he straightened himself up. "The same thing we did when you sang to me last time. Let's get out of here and go find a bed."

"You want more?" she asked, wide-eyed.

"Baby, that was just an appetizer. I'm going for the main course, dessert and a midnight snack. I hope you took your vitamins. You're going to need the strength," he said, and then snatched her little scrap of underwear up from the floor and pocketed it. "I doubt if you can wear them again, but I'm not leaving them here."

"You tore them off of me. You know I can't wear them again."

"Come on. We'll take my car. Is there a back way out of here?" he asked.

"Yes. Come," she said, unlocking the door and heading toward the rear entrance. Suddenly, she stopped. "Did you let Brice and Langston know that you were leaving?"

"Trust me. They know." He smirked.

"Oh, is this some sort of man thing?"

"It's a 'they know the deal' thing," Jarred said, opening her door on his SUV. He helped her in, then hopped into the driver's side.

"Where are we going?"

"My place," he said. "Do you have a problem with that?"

"Of course not. Why would I?"

"Just making sure. You do know you're staying the weekend with me, right?"

"I didn't bring a change of clothes."

"You won't be needing any. I plan to keep you in bed the entire weekend."

She smiled. "Well, this should be interesting."

"Interesting and the best sex and lovemaking you could ever imagine."

"We'll see," she sassed.

"Do I hear a challenge?" he asked.

"Hear whatever you want. After all of the singing and gyrating... I'm just saying."

"Oh, it is definitely on," Jarred growled.

Nevealise laid her head back against the seat and closed her eyes.

"Tired?" Jarred asked.

"Just a little. You?"

"It's been a long week. I'm glad you're back."

"I'm happy to be back. Living out of my suitcase is starting to have its drawbacks." She yawned.

"I could only imagine. Have you been eating properly?"

"Oh yes. And I've slowed down on the energy drinks," she said proudly.

"That's great! Now we just have to teach you how to prepare a proper meal for yourself."

"I guess. I've managed pretty good on my own so far," she said quietly.

"I'm not trying to control you, Nevea. If you're going to keep working like you do, you will need to eat balanced meals or the long days will surely catch up to you. I'm not saying learn how to cook a six-course meal. Just enough to sustain you."

"Thank you for that. You know, I can fix a salad. I just can't cook anything on the stove."

"Salad is good. You don't have to use the stove. A lot of stuff these days is made for the microwave. You'll just have to remember to buy it." He shot her a glance. "I worry about you."

"Aw, that's so sweet," she said happily, and leaned over and kissed him on the cheek.

"Hey, none of that. You're going to make us crash. We'll have plenty of time for all of that once I get you home."

"Umm-hmm," she teased. "Tick tock. Tick tock."

"What are you trying to say?"

"Time's a-ticking, buddy."

"You are full of sass tonight, aren't you?"

"Yep. I can't wait to show you my new moves."

Jarred jerked his head around so fast that he almost lost control of the car.

Nevealise grabbed hold of the dashboard. "Jarred!" she cried. "Are you trying to kill us?"

"Sorry. You can't be saying things like that to me while I'm driving. What moves? And just where did you learn these 'new' moves?" he growled.

"What's wrong with you?" She scowled. "Where do you think I learned them?"

"That's what I'm trying to figure out," he barked. "You haven't been conducting any more experiments, have you?"

Hearing his accusation and seeing the dark look on his face, Nevealise regretted she'd ever told him about her sexual experiment in college. She never dreamed it'd make him think the worst of her. *How dare he!* "If you think so little of me, take me back to Heavens right now! Turn this car around," she shouted.

She couldn't believe Jarred was just like her father—overbearing and full of assumptions. Nevealise had already had one self-righteous, full-of-himself person attached to her life. Her father was more than enough. She didn't need another.

"You're the one who said you learned some new moves. What am I supposed to think?"

She was livid. So much so that her eyes started to water. However, she refused to let him see her shed one bleeping tear. "Take me back to Heavens right now. I mean it, Jarred," she demanded, her tone deadly.

To her relief he didn't say a word; he just turned the car around in that direction.

It took them less than fifteen minutes to return to the club. Before the SUV had come to a full stop, Nevealise was out of it and walking quickly toward her car. As soon as she exited, she let the tears flow, streaming down her face. People were calling to her, but she never turned around. She just got into her car and pulled out of the parking lot.

She drove and didn't stop until she reached her destination, almost two hours later. Nevealise pulled up to the house, got out and hurried up the walkway to ring the bell. The outside light came on and the door opened. Her brother Cedric was standing there. A look of confusion knitted his brow.

"Nev, what's wrong?" he asked as he hurriedly pulled her inside and closed the door behind them. "Are you hurt? Talk to me. What's going on?"

"I hate men!" she bawled. She threw her arms around his neck and let the floodgates open.

"Come now. Let's get you settled. You can tell me all about it, and then I can go beat the bastard who hurt you to a bloody pulp. How about that?"

"You always make me feel good."

"That's what big brothers are for. Making little sisters feel better. Come, let's get a drink while you explain what happened."

"I don't want to talk about it tonight. Can I just crash in your spare bedroom?"

"Sure. I'm guessing you didn't bring an overnight bag. I'll find you something to sleep in. I believe you still have some things here from when you were visiting last time."

She leaned into him as he led her to the guest room, never more grateful for her big brother. He was just what she needed tonight.

"Jarred, what's wrong with Nev? What happened?" Brice demanded as he exited the lounge and saw Nev's car speed out of the lot.

His brother scowled as he sat in his SUV. "Let it go, Brice. Now is definitely not the time," he barked, and screeched out of the parking lot.

Langston winced at the sound. He turned to look at Brice. "How did they go from practically making love onstage to her running out of his car in tears, and Jarred tearing out of here like a man possessed?" he murmured.

"I don't know." Brice shrugged. "He's probably heading home. I'm going after him to see what happened. I need answers. I'll give him the third degree if I have to."

Langston glared at him. "Brice, you sound like the police. Jarred is already in a mood. He doesn't need your temper on top of his. The problem is y'all are too hot-tempered. Always ready to fly off the handle for any little thing. Let's wait to see what's happened before jumping to conclusions."

"I didn't jump to conclusions. I simply want to know what's going on. However, you're right. We both need to calm down. Langston, you know Jarred has serious trust issues. I'm pretty sure he said or did something stupid."

"Who doesn't? From what you and Jarred have said, Nev has the same trust issues. They are both going to have to learn how to deal with them."

"Are you still taking those oneness classes?"

"What? I never took a oneness class." Langston scowled.

"You know, like that place you took Jarred to."

"You and Jarred both can go straight to hell," Langston fumed. "It was getting in touch with one's inner self—back in college. We're all grown-ups now."

"Temper, temper." Brice snickered knowingly, waving his finger back and forth.

"You know, you can be a pain." But never one to stay mad, and certainly not at his brother, Langston laughed, taking the teasing in stride.

"I'm just saying you're not exempt from the temper pool." Brice pulled out his phone. "I'm going to call Nev's cell to see if she's okay," he said, concerned.

Langston waited while Brice dialed Nev's phone and put his on speaker. After the fourth ring her voice mail came on.

"Nev, it's Brice. Give me a call as soon as you get this message."

Langston could tell Brice was upset. He was no longer smiling. In fact, his facial features were tight, his lips clamped together and his body stiff with tension.

"She just left, Brice. She probably can't reach her cell. Honestly, she looked more pissed off than anything else," Langston said quietly. "I'm sure she's okay."

"I'll talk to you tomorrow. I'm going home," Brice said, and walked off in the direction of his car.

Chapter 14

Jarred made it home in record time. He was surprised he hadn't gotten a ticket. He walked through his front door and went directly to the liquor cabinet, where he reached for the Hennessy, opened it and took a big swig directly from the bottle.

"Ugh!" he cried, almost choking on the liquid, which burned his throat as it went down. He brought the bottle back up to his lips and drank again. He repeated his actions until the bottle was empty.

He'd felt the effects of the whiskey after his third swig, but wouldn't stop drinking.

"She's just like that cheating, lying Lainey. All women are alike," he slurred, as he staggered across the room.

Jarred blinked several times, trying to see up the stairs. Everything was blurry. He tried to climb onto the first step, but missed it and fell. From his position on the floor he lifted his hazy gaze again, but could make out only shadows. Reaching for the bannister, he slowly pulled himself up, trying to keep his balance.

"There." He brought his foot down, missed the step again and fell—this time on his face.

"Aw, come on! Stop moving the stairs. You can do it, Jarred," he chanted. When all else failed he crawled up the steps and into his bedroom, where he fell face-down on the bed.

"Ha! You can't beat me." He laughed.

"Night, night," he whispered.

The insistent ringing of his doorbell woke Jarred up out of his alcohol-induced sleep. He'd left Heavens in a state and had come straight home and gotten drunker than he'd been since his college days.

He was paying for it tenfold. The ache that throbbed behind his eyes made him feel as if the top of his head was going to explode. His mouth felt as if he had a bushel of dirty cotton in it. The treacherous ringing and constant banging on his door weren't helping, either.

Jarred staggered out of bed. Somehow he made it downstairs to the door.

"Who is it?" he called, his voice raspy from all the alcohol he'd consumed.

"Langston and Brice. Open the door, bro."

Jarred didn't feel like company. Especially the company of his know-it-all brothers. He contemplated letting them stay outside on his stoop. However, chances were the arrogant Manning brothers would keep making noise until someone called the police.

Deactivating his alarm, he unlocked and opened the door. Both brothers pushed past him and into the house.

"Well, come on in, why don't you," Jarred said sarcastically.

"What's wrong with you?" Brice asked, eyeing him.

Jarred winced. His brother's voice vibrated against his temples as if he had a mini army dancing in his skull.

"Tone it down, please," he groaned, clutching his head.

"Man, you smell like a distillery," Langston said, fanning his hand back and forth in front of him. "Just how much did you have to drink?"

"Too much. I think I may have alcohol poisoning." He grunted, one hand holding his head, the other his stomach. He needed the toilet quick. Jarred had a feeling everything he'd poured into himself last night was getting ready to regurgitate.

"If you were stupid enough to drink that much, then you deserve alcohol poisoning. It's okay to get drunk, but dang, man, are you purposely trying to kill yourself?" Langston demanded.

"Hold that thought," Jarred said, rushing out of the room. He'd barely made it upstairs to the bathroom before he was sick. He stayed there a good ten to fifteen minutes before getting up, washing his face and brushing his teeth.

Jarred stared at himself in the bathroom mirror. He looked horrible. His eyes were bloodshot, and he was still wearing his rumpled clothes from last night.

"I guess this is what all CEOs do," he said to his reflection. Man, after all that, he still felt horrible. The only thing he wanted was his bed.

Jarred went into his bedroom and changed into gym shorts and a T-shirt. He put on his slippers and slowly walked like a robot downstairs to face his annoying brothers.

"Are you okay?" Langston asked.

"I think I'll live. Barely," he added.

The grinding sound of his blender had Jarred wincing in pain again.

"Brice, what the hell are you doing?" he griped, not wanting to talk too loudly. It hurt too much.

"Here, drink this," Brice said grumpily, handing him some concoction that looked just as bad as what he'd emptied in the toilet.

"I am not drinking that. What is it?"

"It'll help with the hangover. Trust me," Brice said.

"Well, it looks like it belongs in some baby's diaper." Jarred frowned, eyeing the concoction suspiciously.

"Drink it down, Jarred. If you don't want to feel miserable for the rest of the day, I suggest you start drinking."

Jarred put the glass to his mouth and tried to drink it all down in one gulp. He couldn't. Interestingly enough, it didn't taste bad. "What's in this?" he asked, finishing off the rest.

"Kale, lemon, ginger, cucumber, pineapple and water," Brice said nonchalantly, as if he were used to making the concoction.

"You two can do whatever you want to for an hour or two. I'm going to stretch out for a bit until the room stops spinning and my stomach settles," he said, turning and walking back up the stairs to his bedroom. As soon as he walked through the door, he kicked off his slippers and fell flat on top of the covers and closed his eyes. He was asleep within minutes.

"Man, he didn't get this bad when Lainey walked out on him," Langston said.

"I know. I was all ready to give him the business until I saw him," Brice said.

"Were you able to reach Nev?" Langston asked.

Brice shook his head. "No. I'm worried about her, too. She looked really upset."

"Yes, she did. Well, we can't get any answers until Jarred wakes up. You want to shoot a few hoops while we wait?"

"We may as well. Come on, Lang, let me show you how to play ball."

"You gon' call me Lang one too many times, little brother."

"Whatever. You still gon' get whooped."

"We shall see."

Jarred opened his eyes for the second time that day and lifted his head. Turning his neck slowly, he realized that his head felt 99 percent better and so did his stomach. Pushing up from the bed, he took out a change of clothes and a clean pair of boxers. He then headed for the shower.

Afterward Jarred made his way down the stairs. He looked around and didn't see his brothers. Maybe they'd left. He doubted it. Jarred walked over to the coffeemaker and started it up.

He ran his hand down his face. What a mess last night had been. What had started out as a great evening had ended in what some would describe as a nightmare. When Nevea had told him she had been practicing moves, he'd seen red. He'd suddenly remembered all the lies Lainey had told him, and how he'd believed every one of them. All the while she and his so-called good friend Braxton had been carrying on behind his back. The sting of betrayal from both of them had cut deep. Braxton was supposed to have been in Jarred's wedding, but instead had ended up marrying the bride-to-be. Jarred was determined never to be taken for a fool like that again.

He turned his head at the sound of voices coming from the basement. Both Langston and Brice were stepping through the door, sweating and squabbling about someone cheating.

"Look, Brice, the dead has arisen," Langston said mockingly.

"So I see. How do you feel?"

"Much better. Thanks," Jarred said.

"I would say let's grill some burgers and have a few beers, but you've had enough drink for all of us," Brice snickered.

"Maybe," he said softly. "We can still throw something on the grill. It's a little breezy, though."

"When has that ever stopped you? You've grilled in the dead of winter," Brice said.

"True. I'll throw a few steaks on. You and Langston can make whatever fixings you want." He took the steaks out of the freezer and walked toward his backyard without saying another word.

"Man, he's hurtin'," Langston said quietly.

"Yeah, he is." Brice's tone was just as quiet.

Jarred started the gas grill and waited for it to warm. He didn't really need to, but he wanted some time to clear his head. His brothers looking at him the way they were took him back to the incident with Lainey.

He looked over at the steaks and realized he hadn't seasoned them. He shook his head and took them back to the kitchen.

"What's wrong?" Langston questioned.

"I need to season these," he said, holding the meat up.

They worked cooperatively. No one said a word other than what was needed for their meal. After everything was prepared they went out to the patio to eat.

"You want to talk about it?" Brice asked.

"Not really, but I will anyway." Jarred sighed and closed his eyes. He opened them and went on to tell his brothers about his and Nevealise's first encounter. Not everything and not in specifics, but he did mention how she'd researched sex in her much-loved books. That sent Langston and Brice into fits of laughter.

"At the time it was funny to me, too. Well, not when she mentioned her experimental partner, when we were…you know. But then as she explained, I understood what she was saying. Last night when she was telling me about these new moves she learned…" He shook his head. "What can I say? I saw red. It took me back to everything that happened with Lainey. I sort of flew off the handle," he murmured, and closed his eyes once more. In his mind he saw her angry face and heard her saying that he was just like her father. It hadn't hit him until just a few minutes ago what she'd meant.

"Did you even ask her what she was talking about?" Brice asked.

"Well…yeah."

"Did you ask, Jarred, or did you yell and accuse?" Langston inquired.

"I don't remember. All I know is there was a whole lot of yelling going on inside my SUV. She demanded that I take her back to Heavens and that's what I did. I'm not sure of anything after that." Jarred grunted. "I was so angry."

"I think you're letting your experience with Lainey cloud your judgment with other women. You really have to let that go. You tell Nev that she needs to let go of her father issue, yet you hold on to your 'woman' issue. It's hypocritical," Langston said.

Jarred realized that his brother was right. He was comparing every woman to Lainey.

"You need to think about this, too," Brice interjected. "If Nev told you she learned how to kiss, and whatever else, from reading and research, did it ever occur to you that she'd researched different ways to please a man?"

Jarred felt as if someone had slapped him in the face. Could she have meant that she'd *read up* on some new moves? Oh damn, he was screwed. He looked from one brother to the other.

"I messed up, didn't I?"

"That would be an affirmative, bro." Brice shrugged.

"I'll just have to fix it," Jarred said.

"Well, good luck with that. Nev has gone for years without speaking to her father, her own flesh and blood. You, Jarred, basically confirmed her view on men," Brice said.

"I still can't get past how you'd think she was anything like Lainey when she's twenty-eight years old and has only had two partners in all that time. Well, one

and a half. The experiment dude just doesn't count."
Langston gave an exaggerated shudder.

"I'll get her back," Jarred said confidently.

"I'm glad you're so sure of yourself, bro," Brice said.

"Well, hopefully, I have an ace." He grinned.

"What?" Langston asked.

"Nevea and I made love several times without a condom. Even last night in her dressing room."

Jarred could have laughed outright at the expressions on his brothers' faces.

"Whoa," Langston murmured.

"Cheers!" Brice smiled and held up his beer. Langston and Jarred followed suit. Only Jarred had a bottle of water.

"We may be smiling now, but if Mom finds out you did something as irresponsible as that, she's going to have your head." Brice smirked.

"You would love that, wouldn't you?" Jarred asked.

"For sure."

"I suggest you work on finding Nev first," Langston advised. "But not too soon. I have a feeling she's going to need some space to cool off."

Chapter 15

Jarred was in a foul mood. He hadn't seen hide nor hair of Nevealise in over a month. He'd staked out her apartment in Cambridge, and Heavens. He'd even gone so far as to ask Mrs. Tempest if she'd heard from her. Mrs. Tempest had said she believed her daughter had gone on a business trip. Jarred couldn't argue with that, since Nevea's job took her to different places all the time. Sometimes for weeks at a time. She'd disconnected her cell phone or changed the number. Either way, neither he nor Brice could get in contact with her.

Jarred looked up at the sound of voices coming from his office doorway. He groaned inwardly. He didn't need anybody right now, but especially not Emerson, Brice and Langston. All three of them parading in here together like they were in some kind of damn marching band only meant there was trouble.

"Doesn't anybody know how to knock in this place?" Jarred grumbled.

"I can see you're sporting that same sunny disposition," Brice said drily.

"Dude, ain't nobody coming to see your grumpy old self but us. You have the entire second floor and most of the first hightailing it in a different direction once they see you coming," Emerson complained. "You should be thanking us for placating your employees. I know a few who are probably thinking up ways for your demise."

"Placating them how?" he questioned.

"Don't bust a gut, Jarred," Brice replied. "Emerson just so happened to send out a memo, informing the employees to excuse your bad behavior—you just needed a friend. He then asked for volunteers," he added nonchalantly.

Jarred's eyes bulged. His mouth flew open, but no sound came out, and he clenched the pen he held so hard it dug into his hand.

"You didn't," he croaked.

"You can relax, bro. Nobody volunteered." Brice snickered.

"You all better have a good reason for being in my office," Jarred snapped.

"We do," Langston said, and sat down. Brice and Emerson followed suit.

Jarred frowned. Neither Brice nor Emerson ever took a seat in the chairs in front of his desk unless Langston did. When they came to see him alone, he'd have to tell them to have a seat. He wondered what their intention was.

"Well, is someone going to start talking or should I take a number?" he asked sarcastically.

"We had something of a breakthrough and thought we'd come by here and discuss it with you."

Jarred sat up straighter in his seat. "What kind of breakthrough?"

"Emerson's spoken to a former senior VP of Tempest," Brice whispered.

"Brice, why are you whispering?" Jarred frowned. "And if Emerson spoke to this person, then why isn't he telling the story?"

"It's not a story," Brice barked, clearly annoyed. "Can I finish?"

"By all means, proceed." Jarred waved his hand.

"First, we need to get into that system. Did you know that the investment companies owned by Josiah are subsidiaries of Tempest Mortgage?" Brice asked, with a smug look on his face.

"What are you talking about? The subsidiaries are not on Tempest Mortgage's corporate papers," Jarred said. "Where did you get that information from?"

"Emerson's contact," Brice stated.

"Emerson, just who is your contact?" Jarred asked.

"As Brice revealed, she's a former employee of Tempest," Emerson said.

"Is she reliable?"

"Very. She practically gave me the rundown on the company from the time she started until the time she left."

Jarred eyed Emerson intently. "She's not some disgruntled employee, is she?"

"No, actually, she was the one who brought it to

Josiah's attention that something fishy was going on," Emerson responded.

"So where is she working now?" Jarred asked, not ready to believe in this ex-employee just yet.

"She's a compliance officer for the SEC." Emerson grinned.

Jarred whistled through his teeth. "And she gave you this information freely?"

"Well, I sure as hell didn't bribe it out of her." Emerson glowered.

"I didn't think you had. I'm just saying she's putting her career on the line by giving you this information. Why would she do that for someone she doesn't know?"

"Because the SEC is about to shut down those investment companies, just as soon as she gives them the final paperwork."

Jarred got a headache right between the eyes. He closed them and pinched the bridge of his nose.

"She's a whistleblower." Jarred shrugged. "I guess you can't get any more reliable than that."

"Exactly, and she needs those files on the computer just as much as we do," Brice chimed in. "If my theory is correct, we may not be in a bad position."

"And your theory is?" Jarred asked.

"Like I said before, the investment companies are subsidiaries of Tempest, but not a part of Tempest."

"How so?" Jarred frowned, not understanding where Brice was going with this.

"The thing is the mortgage company is not under investigation. Because Dad organized this buyout, there wasn't any real background work done on Tempest. I've always known something was fishy. See, we've been going under the assumption that the mortgage company was in the red. Not at all. Honestly, I think it's brilliant how Josiah set this up. It's almost like some exceptional pyramid scheme!" Brice exclaimed.

Jarred put his head down to hide his grin. Brice was so excited. He could hear it in his brother's animated voice, as well as see it in his eyes. Brice looked like a kid who had just received his favorite video game as a present.

"Can you contain yourself a little longer, Brice, and get to the point?" he asked drily.

"Picture this. Tempest Mortgage is at the top. Under the top dog are investment companies one, two and three, so to speak. All three are subsidiaries of top dog. If one, two, three investment companies fold, you still can't touch top dog. Different boards of directors and so forth. If the SEC comes in and shuts down the investment companies, they still can't get top dog. But this was not always the case. Top dog used to be connected. Gets wind of a corporate takeover. Top dog starts putting his plan in motion."

"And just what is that plan?" Jarred asked. Brice had his attention so far.

"Top dog has put dummy people in place to buy up all of his shares in the investment companies."

"First of all, how do you set up dummy people? There are dummy corporations—"

"You need to get Nev off the brain for a second and think," Brice interrupted.

Jarred glared at him so hard that if he were able to shoot laser beams, Brice would be dead.

But his brother was undaunted. "I'm serious. Listen for a second. You construct phony people the same way you would organize a counterfeit corporation. There are a whole lot of deceased people owning things they've never bought. You know this."

"I stand corrected. Go ahead."

"Josiah set a plan in motion whereas the board was paying him to buy himself out. The company is set up like some brilliant pyramid scheme, as I said. You could get to the top but you couldn't take the top company down without destroying yourself in the process. Only Josiah's plan was better."

"I don't follow," Jarred said. "And I still don't understand how all of this is going to help us."

"Bottom line, Josiah put people in charge whom he thought he could trust. Realizing that he's getting older and not in good health, these same people try to overthrow him. Not only that, they're doing underhanded trades, giving loans to unqualified friends and embezzling funds through dummy loans. Josiah is suspicious, has Nev come in to install this software to track activities. No one is the wiser, and if they were…well, there was nothing anyone could do. They couldn't break into the system without being revealed. Tempest is sold. Computers with proof are inherited by the new company. All moneys are in escrow for proof on Josiah's part of no wrongdoing. Investment company people go to jail. The end."

"I have to admit some of what you say makes sense. However, there are a lot of holes in your breakdown. For one thing, it's all supposition. How do we know that's what really happened?" Jarred leaned back in his chair. "Listen, it has already been established that something underhanded was going on," he continued. "We just don't know what, and until we get into those computers, we've hit a brick wall. But if half of what Brice says is true, we're going to dump Tempest quick, fast and in a hurry. I don't want any shady dealings attached to Manning's," Jarred stressed.

"It's not that we can't get into the computers," Emerson answered. "It's that we can only get so far. The computer is designed with a spyware that will kill the entire system if we try to hack into it. That's some high-level firmware."

"What we need is to get Nev in here to help with this," Brice said.

"Just how do you propose we do that, Brice?" Jarred asked, his frustration rising. He pinned him with a stare that could melt stone. "If you can find her and get her back here, then please be my guest."

A sudden quiet permeated the room. No one said anything or moved. It was as if they'd just broached a subject that was completely taboo.

"I have to go out. I'll see you all later," Brice said, getting up and leaving the room. He slammed the door in his wake.

Jarred winced.

"Yeah, I have to go, too," Emerson said, and was up and out the door.

Jarred glanced over at Langston. "I guess you have someplace to be, too?"

"No. Not really," he said, knitting his fingers together and giving Jarred a sympathetic stare. "So, do you want to go get some lunch?"

Jarred couldn't help it. He burst out laughing. "Thanks, man. I'm good."

"Anytime. I'll see you again before the end of the day," Langston said, pushing up from his chair. "It will all work out. Think of it this way. Nev will always return to Heavens."

"I know. The million-dollar question is when?"

Without saying anything else, Langston left the room.

Once Jarred was alone, his office phone rang. He snatched it up.

"Mr. Manning, your father is on line one," his new temp said hesitantly.

"Thank you, Laura. I got it," he said sweetly. It wasn't right for him to be taking his anger out on his employees. "Well, this is a surprise. How are you, Dad?"

"I'm fine. It's you your mother is worried about," he said in his gruff voice.

"Me? Why?"

"Word is all of your employees are about to quit on you."

"An exaggeration at best. Who told you that—Brice or Langston?"

"I will not reveal my sources." He could hear his father's amusement through the phone. "So, is it true?"

"Is what true?"

"That you're being a pain in the you-know-what. That's what."

"No," he said huffily. "Not really."

"What's the problem, son?"

"You mean the Brothers Two didn't tell you?" he asked drily.

"When have you ever known your brothers to betray a confidence? On the other hand, Kat, if you get her mad, will give you away every time," William Manning joked.

They both knew that wasn't true about her. Kat could hold a confidence and a grudge until the next coming.

"I believe I may have screwed up big time," Jarred mumbled, pinching the bridge of his nose.

"How so?"

He went on to give his father a little bit of detail on what was going on with him and Nevea.

"So are you saying you had a thing with Nevealise Tempest?"

"Yes, Dad."

"And you didn't trust her, but you trusted her enough to sleep with her, even after you knew she was basically, for all intents and purposes, innocent in things of that nature?"

"Well…well, it wasn't really like that, Dad." He hesitated.

"How was it? It sounds that way to me. You put your former woman's issues onto your current woman and expected her to come willingly back into your arms."

"Well, Dad, she basically did the same thing," Jarred whined, feeling the need to defend himself.

"Who put her in the position to say those things to you?"

"I did," he said grudgingly.

"That's right, son. You did. That young lady trusted you with her secrets and her body. She gave to you willingly what she hadn't given to anyone else, and you threw it back in her face. Heck, son, I wouldn't speak to you, either."

"Make me feel worse, why don't you," Jarred grumbled, rubbing his temples, his eyes and beard.

"I believe you're doing enough of that yourself. Feeling sorry for yourself, that is."

"There's something else, and don't you dare tell Mom," Jarred whispered into the phone.

"Let me be the judge of what I tell and don't tell my wife. What else could there be?"

"Nevea could be—may be pregnant," Jarred admitted. "We didn't use condoms a few times."

"You mean *you* didn't. Jarred, you're sounding like a regular knight in shining armor, more so by the minute." His father's tone was sarcastic.

"Not funny, Dad."

"No, it's not. Let me see if I have this right. You found a good woman, lost said good woman, and your mother and I may or may not be grandparents. Is that correct?"

"Well, yeah." He groaned deep in his gut.

"Fix this mess, son."

"How can I when I don't know where she is?" he barked, frustrated.

"Mind your tone, young man. You're an attorney. Be resourceful."

"I may be an attorney, but Nevea's a brilliant walking computer. If she doesn't want to be found, she won't be. Did I also tell you she has high government clearance?"

His father's boisterous laughter annoyed him.

"I'm glad someone thinks this is funny," Jarred muttered.

"It'll work out, son. Trust me."

"I hope so. Remember, nothing to Mom until I figure this out."

Obviously, his father took that as his cue.

"Dee," he called out, "your firstborn done went and got a young lady pregnant, and now he can't find her!"

Jarred heard his mother yelling. "What are you carrying on about, Bill? How do you lose a human being? These young people today. Give me that phone and let me talk to my child."

His mother's voice got louder as she came to the phone.

"Jarred, what is your father going on about?" she yelled in his ear.

Jarred put his head down on the desk and banged it a few times. "This can't be happening to me," he chanted as his mother read him the riot act. He should have known his father wouldn't keep a secret from her.

"Tattletale," Jarred muttered.

"What's that, son?" his mother barked.

"Nothing, ma'am."

Chapter 16

Nevealise was still at her brother's home nursing her wounds and what she suspected was the flu. She hadn't the strength most days to do anything, but work on the computer game she was designing on her laptop. Thank goodness she felt better today.

She hadn't gone back to Heavens since that fateful night that she and Jarred had had their blowup, over a month ago. She'd been so depressed, on top of being sick, that she'd put in for a leave of absence from her consulting work. She needed to get herself together, so while at Cedric's she'd continued to work on her program. Nevealise hadn't seen or heard from any of the Mannings in over a month. She had replaced her old cell number with a new one, cutting off all contact with anyone.

Cedric was working most of the day and sometimes

nights as an emergency medicine physician at Stony Brook University Hospital. He'd been there for a few years now. He would soon be leaving SBU to open a private practice with their other brother, Elijah, in Connecticut. Why they chose Connecticut she didn't know. However, she was proud and happy for both her brothers. Elijah and Cedric were the best big brothers a girl could have. Elijah had been gone for a year now, traveling with a missions group to underdeveloped and underprivileged countries, and providing medical care. He would be back in time for the opening of the practice.

"Hey, Nev. How are you feeling today?" She startled upon hearing Cedric's voice as he entered the living room.

"I feel much better today, thanks. I thought you'd already gone to the hospital." She gave him a hesitant smile. She'd been mooching off Cedric for a month now, afraid to go back to her town house in fear of Jarred turning up there. She wasn't ready to face anyone yet. Not until she got her energy back.

"I'm on my way out in a few. Listen, I need to take a sample of urine from you. There's this bug going around and I think you may have picked it up," he said, handing her a specimen cup. "You know what to do, Nev."

"Cedric, I'm not peeing in this cup. That's just nasty," she said, making a face. "Especially for my brother."

"Nev, pee in the cup. Come on, chop-chop. I have to be on call in a little bit."

"I'm not one of your patients, you know," she complained.

"No, because I would instruct my patients to take better care of themselves. You, my dear sister, refuse to listen to reason. Now be a good baby girl and give big brother Cedric your sample."

Nevealise grudgingly complied with his wishes.

"Here," she said, handing him the sealed cup. "I hope you get fired for carrying around urine."

"Ah, don't be like that." He picked up his phone and keys, getting ready to leave, but then turned back to her. "Have you spoken to Mom lately?"

"I sure have. Yesterday."

"So you know the old man is really ill?"

"Yep, I sure do."

"She needs some company now and again, you know."

"I'm having lunch with her later this week, if I'm feeling up to it. I don't want her catching whatever it is I may have."

"Trust me, Mom can't catch what I suspect you have." He chuckled. "It's safe to have lunch with her sooner."

"How do you know? You're holding my sample in your hand. And what's so doggone funny?"

"Oh yeah, the sample. I'd forgotten. I left food for you in the kitchen. Don't wait up for me," he said, then kissed her on the cheek and like a whirlwind was out the door.

Nevealise stared at his retreating form and frowned. Cedric was acting weird. After hovering over her for weeks, he was suddenly walking around with this smirk and being all jolly and what not.

"Hmm, maybe he has a new lady friend?" she said, looking at her computer screen. If that were true she'd have to go back to her place soon. Cedric would need his privacy.

She'd cross that bridge when she came to it. With a shrug of her shoulders she was once again engrossed in her program.

Her cell phone rang and she automatically picked it up. The only people who had her new number were her mother and Cedric, and Cedric had just left the house.

"Hi, Mommy."

"Hi, sweetheart. How are you feeling today?"

"I'm feeling a lot better. How are you doing?"

"Enjoying this weather. I love spring. Not too cold or too hot…"

"And you can play in your flower beds," Nevealise finished for her.

"Oh, God, yes. Your father is sitting out in the garden now."

Nevealise rolled her eyes heavenward. Her mother seemed so happy, she wouldn't ruin it by sucking her teeth, or just coming out and saying that she didn't care. Besides, she didn't have the energy. Considering how her own relationship had just ended, she was not in a position to call her mother out.

"That's nice. I hope he's enjoying his day," she said, and could have choked on that lie.

"Oh yes, dear, he is. In fact, he's the one who asked me to call you."

Surprised, Nevealise halted what she was doing. "Really?" she asked.

"Oh yes. I told him why you'd canceled our lunch date last week. He wanted to know how you were. Are you really feeling better, dear?"

Nevealise smiled at the concern in her mother's

voice. Her eyes teared up. "Yes, Mommy. I'm just a little tired," she whimpered.

"Then why are you crying?"

"Uh, I haven't a clue as to why I'm crying." She chuckled through a sob. Nevealise's smile broadened when she heard her mother's soft laughter.

"That's okay, dear. Everyone deserves a good cry once in a while."

"I guess so. So are we on for lunch sometime this week?"

"Sure. You let me know when. We'll make a day of it."

"I'd love that," she said sincerely.

"Good. I have to go to a church meeting. I'll talk to you soon, dear."

"Bye, Mommy."

Nevealise returned to her laptop, working on a glitch in the program design of her video game.

She spent a few hours on it before closing her computer down. She worked out the kinks in her neck, but her arms and legs were stiff, too. Standing, she was surprised to find her legs were shaky. Probably she'd been sitting for too long.

Nevealise walked into the kitchen to retrieve the food Cedric had left her. She loved her brother, but the chicken salad he'd left her just didn't appeal to her, so she put it back in the refrigerator, choosing a frozen burrito instead and cooking it in the microwave. Once the microwave dinged, she grabbed her burrito and a cola and sat at the butcher-block counter to eat.

She ran her gaze around the spacious kitchen and sighed heavily. Cedric's house was beautiful, but it was too dang quiet. There wasn't the hustle and bustle of people and traffic in his cul-de-sac. Her thoughts instantly went back to Jarred's kitchen and the first time she'd gone to his house. He'd been a gracious host. She missed him so much. He actually brought balance to her crazy world. Those hazel eyes and athletic body could make any woman swoon.

Thinking of him made her recall their last night together. He'd never given her any indication that he could sing. The night at Heavens when he'd sung "Sex Therapy," his performance had been swoon-worthy. She'd practically melted at his feet. The night had also made her sad, when she'd run from him in tears.

Her girlhood crush had become a reality. She'd made love to Jarred Manning, just as she'd always dreamed. But now she'd lost him, not once, but twice. No matter how she tried to file away her feelings or categorize them, the results were the same. She was in love with him.

With that realization, Nevealise burst out crying. She ran to the bedroom and cried herself to sleep.

Nevealise sat looking at her brother. Her mouth hung open from shock. "What do you mean, I'm pregnant? How do you know that?"

She'd been fast asleep when he'd gotten in. Cedric claimed he'd woken her so she could eat. A lie. He wanted to drop this bombshell on her.

"I suspected it even if you didn't have a clue," he said, his smile gentle. "I didn't want to alarm you just in case I was wrong. I was pretty sure that I wasn't. That's why I asked you for the sample."

"You sneaky snake," she said with a scowl.

"I kept hinting, but you just weren't catching on.

You dive into that laptop of yours and lose all sense of time and anything else. I just let you be. Why do you think I was making sure you ate a healthy meal three times a day, hmm?"

"I don't know! Jarred did that all that time. He claimed that I didn't eat properly," she said, throwing up her hands in annoyance.

"He's right, you don't. You need to start taking better care of yourself, Nev."

"I don't know how you expected me to know I was pregnant." She grimaced just saying the word.

"Nev, when was your last period?"

"I have no clue. It comes when it comes and it goes when it goes. I'm usually so busy that I honestly don't notice. I don't cramp, I only get a little twinge a day or two before it shows, and that's how I judge when to... whatever," she frowned.

"Nev, with all the research you do and books you read, it never once occurred to you to read up on the female body?"

"I know my body, doofus! As far as research, well, that was only to learn how to have sex. You know, the different positions," she rushed to add.

"Jesus saves, Nev," Cedric murmured, placing his face in his hands. "I love our mother to the moon and beyond, but she did you a disservice. She spent so much time trying to keep you from following in her footsteps that she failed to teach you the basic stuff a young woman should know."

"In her defense, I was never interested. I learned some stuff. It's... I've been so busy I kind of just forgot about the basics." Nev shrugged. "I knew that Jarred and I didn't use a condom a few times, but I never once entertained the possibility of getting pregnant. I'm not totally clueless. I knew that I could get pregnant, but not that I would. Does that make sense?"

"Surprisingly, it does," Cedric assured her.

She shook her head. "I guess my internal clock has been operating on so many different times zones lately that I just didn't notice anything different. Now that I'm grounded at home, I just wanted to catch up on sleep."

Nevealise paused when she heard the doorbell ring. "Are you expecting company, Cedric?"

"I'm not. I have no clue who that is."

"I'll stay out of your way, then. I can finish up what I'm doing in my room… I mean the guest bedroom," she said, turning to walk away.

"Don't be silly. You don't have to leave. We don't even know who it is. Seriously, stay where you are. I'll get rid of whoever it is. It's probably one of the neighbors, anyway."

"If you're sure."

"Positive," he said, turning and leaving the room.

Nevealise heard the voice before she saw the man.

"Nev, look who I found," Cedric was saying.

Who in the world had he found and why were they lost? Nevealise thought.

Cedric was walking toward her, Brice in step with him.

"Brice!" she shrieked, and almost did a flying leap into his arms.

"Whoa, Nev!" he exclaimed, laughing, while at the same time engulfing her in a hug.

"What are you doing here?"

"Looking for you," he said.

"Me?" She raised her brows. "Why?"

"Don't be trying to play dumb with me, Nev. You know you did a disappearing act," he declared. "We'll discuss your bad decision making later. That's not why I'm here."

"Is Jarred okay?" she asked anxiously. "Oh, Lord! What happened?"

"Calm down," Brice said softly. "You really love him, don't you?"

Nevealise didn't confirm or deny the question. Instead she lowered her head.

"There's nothing wrong with my brother other than having a bad attitude and driving the office staff crazy. That's not why I'm here. I came by to see you, and ask a favor."

"Oh?" She frowned.

"Should I be insulted?" he teased.

"No, silly. You know I'm always happy to see you," she said. "Come on into the den and have a seat."

"I have to go back to the hospital. An emergency," Cedric said. "Don't wait up for me, Nev. Brice, man, it was nice seeing you again. Don't be a stranger."

"Nice seeing you again, too, Cedric. It's been a long time," Brice said, and gave Cedric dap.

Nevealise watched as Cedric left, then she turned to Brice in time to hear his plea.

"Nev, I need your help," he said. "*We* need your help."

Chapter 17

Jarred walked past his assistant's desk and frowned. Laura had a smile on her face. *What was she smiling about?* Usually, she'd find something to do the moment he came toward her.

"Good morning!" Her smiled brightened. Jarred was taken aback.

"Uh, good morning," he grumbled, and proceeded to his office.

Jarred stopped dead in his tracks. Sitting in one of the wingback chairs in front of his desk was Nevea. Brice was seated on one side of her, Langston on the other, and Emerson was half standing, half sitting on the desk.

"Emerson, get off of my desk," he said gruffly, walking around him to take his seat. His gaze zeroed in on Nevea and stayed there. She was wringing her hands together just like she'd been doing when she showed up at his house that first time.

"Brice said you all needed my help with a computer system," she said nervously.

"We do. Yes." Jarred's heart was pumping so fast in his chest he could scarcely speak. He didn't wish to make a fool of himself in front of his brothers, but he wanted to run to her and hold her. He'd missed her so damned much.

"Where do you need me to start?" she asked.

"The computers are in the Security room," Emerson said.

"Well, let's get started," she said quietly, making a move to get up, and then shaking her head as if to clear the cobwebs.

Jarred shot Langston a quick look.

"Hold on a second, Nev. We have to make sure the room is clear," Langston said. "Come on, fellows."

Jarred was grateful that they didn't ask questions, but just left. He waited for the door to close before he spoke.

"Nevea, are you okay, love?"

"Can I have some water, please?" she croaked.

"You don't look so hot. Are you sure you're okay?" he asked, coming from behind his desk to take her hand. It trembled in his.

"I just need some water."

"Coming up," he whispered, and then rushed over to his minifridge, grabbed a bottle and handed it to her. She looked as if she was going to be sick so he made his way to the bathroom off his office, wet a towel and brought it back to her. He dabbed her face with the wet cloth. "Is that better?"

"A little. Not much," she murmured.

"Do you need something else? What's wrong?"

"My stomach's a little queasy. I'll be okay in a minute."

"Did you eat anything today?"

She shook her head.

"Well, maybe you need to put something—"

"Jarred, I need the restroom. Now," she interrupted.

Jarred deftly lifted her in his arms, rushed her over to the bathroom and placed her on her feet. He'd barely set her down before she was leaning over the toilet, vomiting. He held her hair back from her face and placed the cold cloth on her neck. Tears were running down her face in earnest now.

"Sweetheart, don't cry. It's okay," he soothed.

She lifted her head, went to say something, but then was sick again.

Jarred comforted her until she'd finished. He helped her up.

"How do you feel now?"

"Much better. Tired. You wouldn't happen to have an extra toothbrush in here, would you?" she asked shyly.

"Of course. It's in the vanity. There's also mouthwash. I'm here late a lot recently. I make sure to keep it stocked," Jarred said, handing her everything she needed. Once she was done, he walked her over to the sofa and guided her down. "Would you like your water now?"

"Not really. Do you have a seltzer or something? Ginger ale or Sprite does the trick, too."

"I only have cola, juice and water," he said, eyeing her suspiciously. She was as pale as a ghost.

"Give me the cola," she groaned.

"You're going to be sick again?" He panicked.

"I don't think so. My stomach's still not settled, though."

"Stretch out on the sofa and relax until your belly settles. You can't work sick, anyway."

"Okay," she said, and stretched out. One hand covered her abdomen in a protective way, the other her face.

Jarred heartstrings tugged. Nestled in her belly was their unborn child. Of course, she hadn't verbally confirmed anything, but he knew.

"You wouldn't happen to have a burrito, would you?" she murmured sleepily.

Jarred grinned. "That I don't have."

"Bummer," she whispered. "If you don't mind, I'm just going to close my eyes for a second."

"Go ahead," he said. "I'll be over at my desk getting some work done."

"Okay."

Jarred stood there and watched her until he saw the soft rise and fall of her chest. He walked over to his desk and sat down. A slow smile inched across his face. She was pregnant with his baby. Jarred had to admit he was ecstatic about the baby. Granted, he'd never pictured himself as a father at this stage in his life. He figured he had a lot of time for marriage and parenthood. However, the thought of a little life growing inside Nevea, a little being that he'd taken part in creating, had him feeling all gooey inside.

At the soft knock on his door he rushed across the carpeted floor to answer it. Nevea had just fallen asleep; he didn't want to wake her up. Jarred quietly pulled the door open and ushered Brice and Langston in. He'd figured they would be back.

"How is she?" Langston asked.

"Not good," Jarred whispered. "She can't hold anything down."

Brice frowned. "I had to pull over this morning to let her be sick."

"Where did you find her?" Jarred asked him.

"Her brother Cedric's house. And your tab is growing by the day."

"How'd you know to look there?"

"I didn't. I took a chance. I remembered she used to stay with him a lot to keep from driving back to Cambridge."

"Thank you," Jarred said.

"Well, you don't have to wonder anymore if she's pregnant, that's for sure," Langston whispered.

"No, I don't. She hasn't said anything, but I know. I wish there was something I could do for her. She was so sick she was crying."

"I can't help you with that. I don't have a pregnant girlfriend." Brice shrugged.

"Bye, fool," Jarred teased. "Oh yeah, she says burritos help. If someone can find me a few and some ginger ale, I'd be grateful."

"Will do," Langston said, and he and Brice both left.

Instead of going back to his desk, Jarred pulled a chair up to the sofa and watched her sleep. He sent up a silent prayer of thanks. He'd been given a second chance with her. He refused to mess it up.

Jarred noticed the dark circles beneath her eyes. He didn't like it. He had a feeling she wasn't resting properly. He planned on taking care of that. Just as soon as he could arrange it, he was taking her to the Hamptons for some rest and relaxation. That was if he could convince her to go with him.

She didn't look pregnant to him. She had on a pair of jeans, flats and her signature T. Her hair was pinned up; her face was devoid of makeup. The only difference in her usual casual style was that she wasn't wearing her glasses.

He tilted his head to the side to see if he could see a baby bump. Nope. Nothing.

Jarred sat and watched her for about twenty minutes longer before getting back to work. He had a lot of paperwork to get through if he was going to whisk her off to the Hamptons.

Nevealise came awake slowly. Squinting her eyes, she turned her head, trying to gauge her surroundings and figure out where she was. She felt the soft leather of the sofa beneath her.

"How are you feeling?"

She whipped her head around to look into the handsome face of Jarred. Now she remembered. She was at Manning Enterprises. Brice had brought her here this morning to help with their computer issue.

Nevealise found herself staring at Jarred. Her eyes ate him up, taking in every inch of him. Earlier she'd felt so sick she couldn't absorb his presence. Her stomach fluttered, but not from the sickness that had plagued her earlier. This time it was from pure want.

"Nevea, are you okay?" she heard him ask again. Nevealise wanted to respond. Her mouth opened, but no sound emerged. Her eyes were fixed on him.

She heard him call her for the third time.

"I'm fine," she said hoarsely. At least her tongue was finally moving.

"Do you think you can eat something?"

"I don't know yet," she said, slowly pushing herself into a sitting position on the sofa. She inhaled and then exhaled. Her stomach felt better. "I'm not really hungry. I guess I should try to eat something, anyway."

"Most definitely. It's lunchtime."

"Good Lord! How long have I been asleep?" Her eyes searched his office frantically for a clock.

"Not long at all. Only a couple of hours."

"A couple of hours," she cried, horrified. He'd said "not long" as if she had been sleeping for a mere fifteen minutes. She sighed. Surely they had all guessed her predicament by now. First, she'd been sick in the car ride over here, then again in Jarred's office. The Manning men were not stupid. Oh well, as her friend Jasmine used to say, "no use crying over spilled milk."

Nev calmed herself, telling herself it was time to get down to business. "Are they ready for me to check the computer?"

"Are you sure you're up to it?"

"I feel fine now." She stretched and then yawned. Jarred didn't look convinced. "Honest."

He still didn't look persuaded. "Sounds like you need a few more hours of sleep."

"Please, if I don't get up, I will sleep all day."

"I found you some burritos, ginger ale and crackers."

Nevealise looked at him in surprise. "You did?"

"Yes. Why are you acting so shocked?"

"Because you made fun of my burritos and chips before."

"No, I didn't. I said that wasn't a two-day meal.

Hell, it's not even a one-day meal. But if a burrito is going to keep you from puking up your insides, by all means, eat away."

"Thank you," she said, and beamed at him.

Chapter 18

Jarred watched Nevea intently as she typed away on the computer keys. He was glad that she was feeling better. He'd made sure that she'd eaten some crackers and drunk some of the ginger ale before meeting Langston, Brice and Emerson in the Security room.

As she worked Nevea was muttering what seemed like a bunch of sequential numbers mixed with letters. It all sounded foreign to him.

She had two computers sitting side by side. Jarred couldn't tell if they were feeding off each other or working independently.

Nevea was totally focused on what she was doing, and she looked good doing it.

"Jarred, do you have a private printer in your office separate from the corporate networked computers?" she called out, still typing away.

"No. Why?" He continued to gaze at her. He was both interested in what she was doing and checking for signs that she was going to be sick again or was too tired to continue. At the slightest inkling of either, Jarred was going to pull her away from that computer. By the look of things, she appeared to be in her element. Having fun talking to herself and the monitor.

"Got it," she called out. "One down. I'll need to hide the IP address. Hmm, someone's been naughty."

"Nevea, why do you need a separate printer?" he asked her again, this time more forcefully. She was getting lost in what she was doing. He could see why Nevealise consulted for the big agencies. She was good. Damn good.

"I need to send you some info. I don't want it networked in. It's private," she answered, but her eyes never met his. She held a piece of paper in one hand, reading it, while the fingers of her other hand punched in numbers like she was a machine. He'd had his fair share of outstanding administrative assistants and knew some could type up to one hundred words per minute, but he'd never witnessed it done with one hand. Jarred was in awe of her.

"The Security office has a private printer," Emerson chimed in, breaking into his thoughts.

"No. Not a good idea," she said. "Anyone can get to the info."

"Not from here. This is my office. It's separate from the other Security office. No one has access but the people currently in this room," Emerson said.

"That's good to know." She turned and flashed Emerson a smile before going back to what she was doing.

"She's amazing," Jarred heard Emerson declare.

"What's she saying?" Langston asked, nudging him.

Jarred shrugged. "I haven't the foggiest idea." He really didn't. She would ask either herself or the computer a question, and then promptly answer it. He shook his head and laughed silently to himself. He was in love with a real techy.

Love? Where did that come from? Did he love her?

Jarred had known Nevea for a shorter time than he had known and dated Lainey. Yet his feelings for Nevea were different. Not forced. They came as naturally as he breathed in air. If that was an indication of love, then, yes, he suspected that he was in love with her.

"She's coding it out," both Brice and Emerson said at once.

"Coding what out?" Jarred asked, confused. He had been so engrossed in his own thoughts that he had apparently missed the conversation.

"Langston asked what she was doing, and we told him. Pay attention, bro," Brice said.

Jarred caught his knowing look. He knew he'd been busted, staring at Nevea, and he didn't care. Not one bit.

He turned his attention back to her when she let out a delighted cry. "Here we go," she said, and everyone in the room gathered around her.

"You got in?" Jarred asked excitedly. From the expression on Nevea's face, he knew it was good news. She was grinning from ear to ear.

"Two down," she muttered, her excitement growing, her fingers sprinting across the keyboard.

"I'm in!" she shrieked, and then jumped up and did a little shimmy.

A slow smile spread across Jarred's face. *Well, I'll*

be damned. She did it. He was so proud of her. His lady knew her stuff.

"Nevea, sweetheart, you broke the code?" He asked the question, but already knew the answer. He just wanted to hear her say it. Hear the enthusiasm in her voice.

"Broke it to pieces. *Boom!*" She giggled.

All Jarred could see were lines and lines of blue and green names and numbers scrolling down the screen.

"What is that?" he asked, looking closely at the computer. The bars on the monitor were rolling by too quickly for him to get an idea of what he was looking at.

"It looks like transactions, dates, a lot of names and numbers. It was hidden, and I'm assuming it's important. Plus it's a big file," she said. "If you're going to print it…well, you all know what to do from here. My job is done."

"And what a wonderful job you've done," Jarred declared, not able to hide the pride he felt in her. He turned to face her. She was still beaming with joy. Happiness was written all over her face, and that made him happy. Even though she'd vowed not to help with anything concerning her father, she'd been selfless and had come in even while feeling sick to assist them.

"Whoever installed that other software is high tech. It didn't break my system but it made it hard to get into the new one overlapping the one that I installed. A very clever move indeed."

Their eyes met and held. Jarred didn't bother masking his desire for her. He wanted her badly. He knew it and so did she. He'd caught her eyeing him in his office earlier with the same intensity he now held her captive with. Jarred hadn't said anything then, for fear of her bolting.

He knew they had a lot to discuss. He also knew the office was not the place to do it. No, he needed to get out of here and take her someplace more private. Besides, he just needed to be alone with her—hold her in his arms away from the watchful eyes of his family. Now that she was back, Jarred didn't plan on letting her go again. And he needed to apologize to her for the appalling way that he'd treated her their last night together.

"Emerson, you, Brice and Langston can handle things from here. Nevea needs a break. She's been at this for a couple of hours," Jarred told them. Not that they were paying attention. Their eyes were glued to the computer. He could have waltzed out of the room with Nevea in his arms and the three of them wouldn't have noticed.

Taking Nevea by the hand, he led her out of the office and back up to his. Once they were off the elevator, the stares of his employees weren't lost on him. But he didn't care if the whole world knew that Nevea was his woman. Even if she didn't know it herself. She would soon enough. He planned on correcting a lot of misunderstandings and bad actions that had taken place.

"Other than your 'eloquent' burrito cuisine," he jested, "what do you fancy eating?"

"A burger and fries," she said, without hesitation.

"You had that one ready and waiting, didn't you?" He chuckled. "Do you want to go out someplace local, or have it delivered?"

"Out. I need some air."

"Feeling sick again?" he asked, eyeing her with concern.

"Not at all." She shook her head.

"Okay. Let me grab my cell and we can be on our way," he said, walking into his office and taking his phone out of his desk drawer. He'd put it there before they'd gone down to Security, because he didn't want any interruptions.

"I need to grab my purse, too," she murmured.

He released her hand long enough for her to retrieve her things, and then took hold of it again. "Ready?"

"Ready. Where are we going?"

"There's this pub a few blocks up that makes a great burger. They're pretty quick with preparation, too," he said, walking back to the bank of elevators and taking the waiting car to the first floor. He walked hand-in-hand with Nevea out of the building. It was where she was meant to be.

Chapter 19

Nevealise breathed in the fresh air once they left the confines of the office building. She tried to remove her hand from Jarred's, but he wasn't having it.

"Feel better?" he asked.

"Yes," she said quietly. Now that they were alone she'd become suddenly self-conscious.

"What's wrong? You've gone quiet on me."

"Have I?" She didn't know what he wanted her to say. Other than to announce that she was pregnant—something she wasn't ready to do, even if she did suspect that he already knew. She needed time to process the fact herself. She'd just found out herself yesterday. Plus she didn't know if she could trust him. She'd done so once and he'd turned it back on her.

His husky voice cut into her thoughts. "What are you thinking?"

"That I'm suddenly hungry," she lied.

"The pub is not much farther."

It didn't bother her. The walk would do her good. The mild May afternoon was perfect. Not hot at all. She would take the seventy-degree weather any day, over the hot and muggy days of summer.

As they strolled along the sidewalk, Nevealise took note of the shops, the different restaurants and vendors. Unlike the peacefulness of her brother's place, the streets of Manhattan were bustling with people. It didn't bother her that everyone was rushing to be somewhere.

"Do you drive into the office or take the train?" she asked Jarred, for no other reason than to spark a conversation.

"Drive most days. I don't like a lot of people in my personal space."

Nevealise smiled. She could understand that. His everyday surroundings were so spacious that being on a crowded train could be a problem.

"But it's easier to take the train, right?" she asked.

"Sometimes. I still prefer to drive. Buses and trains come in handy during the snowy winter months."

"I prefer trains, but they can be a hassle in Boston if you don't know how they run. When I'm in Cambridge, I try to walk wherever I need to go."

"This is the place," Jarred said, stepping aside and allowing her to precede him in.

"Thank you," she said, walking through the door.

Nevealise looked around. The "pub" was a little mom-and-pop place with a quaint feel to it. There was friendly banter happening throughout the establishment, leading her to believe that most of the customers were regulars. Her gaze traveled the expanse of the front area where she and Jarred stood. She noticed the many dishes of food on the customers' tables, which all looked divine.

"Do you want anything on your burger?" Jarred asked.

"The works, with fries and pickles," she responded.

"And to drink?"

"A seltzer water."

She waited with him while he placed their orders. Then they found a two-person table toward the back and took their seats. Jarred held her chair and waited for her to sit before he joined her.

"They'll have our food ready soon," he said.

"Suddenly, I'm starving."

"You should be. It's going on four o'clock in the afternoon and you've only had a few crackers and a soda," he said.

"Wow, that late?" she asked, her eyes wide. "No wonder I'm starting to feel tired."

"Are you sure you're up to this?" he asked.

"I'm fine, Jarred."

"Would you tell me if you weren't?" he inquired softly.

"Of course. Why wouldn't I?"

"I was just wondering. I didn't want to presume anything. By the way, thanks for helping us with that computer problem. We've been at our wits' end trying to get into that system."

"No problem. It was relatively easy, because I designed some of the firmware. I was surprised that my father had used some of my information to open certain files," she said. Surprised was a mild description for how she'd felt upon that discovery. Evidently she was good for something in his eyes.

"Hmm. Interesting."

"Very," she said, and moved back a little as the young waiter brought their food to the table.

"This looks scrumptious!" she said. "But there's no way in the world I'm going to be able to eat all of it."

"Eat what you can. If you like it well enough you can take the leftovers home for later," Jarred said, biting into his burger.

Nevealise had to use her knife to cut her burger in half, and still had a hard time fitting it into her mouth. She bit down into it, savoring the flavor.

"Good?" Jarred asked around a mouthful of his food.

"Yes," she mumbled, and then reached over, took a french fry from the basket and popped it into her mouth. "Unbelievably so."

She was enjoying her food, but all too quickly she felt full. She didn't want to overdo it. Her stomach was being nice to her now. She wasn't going to purposely do anything to upset it. When she started to feel a rumbling sensation, she opened her seltzer water and took a swig. That seemed to do the trick.

"Stomach bothering you?"

Nevealise started. *What was he, a mind reader or something?* "Not really," she replied. The food she'd so fervently wanted she now looked at with disdain.

"Do you want to take the rest with you?" Jarred asked.

Nevealise wanted to, but knew she'd just dump it later on. Her stomach was always playing tricks on her, she realized, suddenly feeling miserable. The fact that she couldn't eat much shouldn't bother her the way it did, but her eyes watered on their own accord. She quickly lowered her head. However, she couldn't stop the lone tear that escaped. The droplet landed on her hand.

"Nevea, what's wrong?" Jarred asked anxiously. She could hear the panic in his voice.

She hadn't meant to alarm him. Her emotions were all over the place lately. Still, she didn't speak, for fear of losing it and breaking down in front of him.

Jarred went to get up, but she gestured with her hand for him to stop. "Please don't," she whispered. "I don't want to embarrass us both by drawing attention to myself," she murmured.

"What happened?" he asked softly. She could still hear the concern in his voice.

Nevealise drew a deep breath, took the napkin off her tray and dabbed discreetly at her eyes. "Nothing," she croaked. "Absolutely nothing. Lately, I've been crying for any little old thing. Don't worry about it. Finish your food, Jarred." For lack of something better to do, Nevealise picked up one of her fries and took a small bite, chewing it slowly. What was so delicious minutes ago now tasted like cardboard.

"Don't," he whispered.

"Wh-what?" she questioned.

"You're going to make yourself sick. Don't force yourself to eat."

She dropped the half-eaten fry back into the basket and heaved a sigh of frustration. "I just didn't want to waste all of this."

"I told you we can take it to go," he said calmly. "Are you ready?"

"No. Finish your food, Jarred. I'll be fine." She cleared her throat and took a sip of her seltzer.

"Nev—"

"Please." She stated firmly.

"If you're sure," he said, and began to eat the rest of his meal with fervor, and then finish off his soda in just about one gulp.

"Goodness, someone was hungry and thirsty," she joked, trying to lighten the suddenly tense atmosphere.

"I guess I was." He chuckled, looking down at his empty plate and glass.

"I wish I could have enjoyed my burger as much as you," she murmured sadly.

"You will again. Soon. Your being sick will pass quickly," he said sympathetically. Her head shot up, her eyes darting to his face. *He knows.* Or so she thought. However, by looking at him she couldn't tell. He gave no indication that he was aware of her condition. Only innuendos. His face appeared devoid of emotion.

When his cell began to ring, he took it out and scowled down at it.

"Excuse me a minute, Nevea," he said, and answered.

"We'll be back shortly," he said to whoever was on the line.

Nevealise lowered her head, trying not to listen to his conversation. She didn't have to try too hard, one-sided as it was. She was able to hear only his responses, not the questions.

"I'll talk to you this evening," he said, right before he ended the call. "That was Brice," he told her. "Apparently they took their faces away from the computer long enough to notice that we weren't there," he added sarcastically.

"They've just noticed now?"

"Unbelievable, right?" Jarred said drily, garnering a chuckle from her.

"And here I thought that I get lost in my work."

He laughed, then said, "Ready to go?"

"I'm ready," she said. The sudden onslaught of different smells filling her nostrils was bringing on a bout of nausea. She watched as Jarred raised his hand to get a server's attention.

"The lady wants to take that with her," he said, pointing to her leftovers.

"Sure. I'll be right back," the young man said. A few minutes later he returned with a take-out box.

"Jarred, do you know if there's a restroom here?" Nevealise didn't usually use public facilities, but in this instance she didn't have a choice.

"I'm positive there is." When he saw her put her hand on her belly, his gaze darted around. Her eyes followed his anxiously. She was hoping he'd find one quickly.

"Come on," he said. Jarred grabbed her by the hand and rushed to the other side of the pub. She had to hold on to her handbag to keep from it falling as he led her to the restroom. He pushed the door open and she ran inside.

Nevealise was grateful for the privacy there. She ran to the first stall, barely making it before she was sick once more. *That's it. I'm never eating anything again.* Groaning, she flushed the toilet, and then washed up, popping a mint in her mouth.

Jarred was waiting anxiously by the ladies' room door, his face taut with worry.

"Are you okay, sweetheart?" he asked softly.

Ah, he called me sweetheart. She caught herself from going into another crying spell.

"Let's get out of here," he said, taking her hand and walking briskly out of the pub.

But as they dashed along the crowded New York City sidewalk, she couldn't hold it in a minute longer.

"Jarred, I'm pregnant," she blurted out.

She didn't know what she expected his reaction to be, but it wasn't what she got.

"Yes, I know, love." He merely flashed her a smile and led her down the street.

Chapter 20

He was at his wits' end. Nevea had revealed to him almost two weeks ago that she was pregnant. Yet she'd refused to go back to his place with him. Instead, he'd had to drop her at her brother's house, after promising not to say anything to his family. According to her, she "needed time to process everything." As if his family didn't know already. And process what? She was having a baby, not a damn computer chip. Not only that, she'd refused to discuss the subject with him, spouting off some lame excuse.

He was royally pissed. Their ten-minute nightly talks weren't nearly enough. He needed to know that she was okay, and taking care of herself properly.

Just how long was she planning on holding his little slip against him?

Jarred was tired and horny as hell. He wanted his

Nevea back. Just the thought of slipping between her thighs almost sent him over the edge plenty of nights. Instead of watching her belly swell with his baby, he was relegated to the sidelines.

He looked around his plush office and wanted to throw something. What, he didn't know. Just something. He'd been holed up in here more now than ever before. He shouldn't mind, really. There was nothing and no one waiting for him at home. His sanctuary was fast becoming his den of depression.

His brothers had taunted him about his melancholy mood, saying that they preferred him barking at them rather than him being holed up in his office looking like a lost puppy. He owed them a beat-down for the lost-puppy crack.

There was a knock of three quick taps at Jarred's office door. Langston. That was his signature knock. Jarred smiled. His middle brother was a lot like him in many ways, although Langston had always been the calmest of the three brothers. He saw reason where Jarred and Brice didn't.

"Come in, Langston," he called out. The door opened and Langston strutted in with purpose. Jarred noticed the huge file he was carrying and wondered what it contained. It couldn't involve bad news because his brother's features were too relaxed. A few months ago they'd been the polar opposite. "What's up?"

"Nothing really," Langston said, taking a seat.

"What's in there?"

Jarred watched as Langston looked down at the file in his hand as if he'd forgotten he was holding it. Jarred didn't know how that could be. The file looked to be the size of a small baby. *Baby.* Jarred's stomach clenched.

"Oh." Langston frowned down at his package. "These are some of the documents recovered from the computer. I was reading over them."

"Anything interesting? I mean, apart from the obvious?"

"Not so far. I'm meeting with that SEC lady next week. I want to make sure I don't give her something to hang us with," Langston said in a nonchalant manner.

"I thought Emerson was handling that?" Jarred inquired, lifting an eyebrow.

"The only day she can meet is on a day that Emerson has a school trip with Jessica. So I agreed to go in his stead." Langston shrugged.

Jarred's face lit up in a smile at the mention of Emerson's ten-year-old daughter, who had taken to calling him and his brothers "uncle." His smile widened at the thought of Jessica having a little cousin to fuss over.

"What are you smiling about?" Langston asked, cutting into Jarred's thoughts.

"Little Jessica," he responded, not offering up any other information on where his thoughts had gone. As usual, to Nevea.

"Little Jessica is not so little anymore," Langston said drily. "She had the nerve to tell me that her friends think I'm a 'hottie,' and then offered to fix me up with one of their mothers."

Jarred laughed heartily. "When was this?" he asked around peals of laughter.

"I took her to dinner last week. We haven't been seeing much of her lately."

"That was nice of you. I have to get over there to see her, too, after I get this thing with Nevea straightened out," he murmured. Hopefully, it would be soon.

He was tired of the lonely feeling in the pit of his gut. He wanted his woman back.

Jarred hadn't realized that he'd gone silent on Langston until he heard his brother asking, "Have you heard from her?"

"Yes. I speak to her every day for about ten minutes at a time," he responded with a heavy sigh. Saying it out loud caused him even more despair.

"Once a day?" Langston inquired.

"No, once in the morning and then at night. Sometimes," he added. Annoyed, Jarred, rocked back in his chair and threw the pen he was holding down on his desk. "May as well be once a day. What the hell is ten minutes? I don't understand why she's being so unreasonable," he muttered.

"Have you done anything, other than whine, to make her want to talk to you more often?"

"What do you mean?" He scowled.

"Just what I said. Do you do anything to make her want to be with you?" Langston stressed.

"Yes, I do. I call her. I text her three times a day to make sure she's eating properly. What else am I supposed to do?" he asked, throwing up his hands in frustration.

"Step up your game, bro." Langston laughed quietly.

Jarred glared at him. "I am so happy that my situation is amusing you."

"Not the situation. You. You're amusing me. I mean, you're running a multimillion-dollar corporation. You head department meetings, as well as board meetings, like a champ, and this business with Dad and Tempest. Even though it's frustrating, you're still handling it like a pro. And don't think that Brice and I don't know you come back to this office to work even after you've supposedly gone home. Yet you're sitting here sulking like you don't know how to get your woman back. A woman, I might add, who is pregnant with your child," Langston said, leaning forward for emphasis. "Man, you've had to deal with corporate mergers that were ten times harder than this situation."

Jarred had no idea his brothers knew that he often came back to the office to get work done. Sometimes until two o'clock in the morning. What they didn't know was that he'd started doing that to occupy his thoughts and time after Lainey had called off the wedding. But as time went on, it was just something he thought he had to do to keep things running smoothly with the company. Especially after they'd started acquiring more businesses. Just when he'd started to relax, go home at a decent hour and on occasion enjoy the company of a woman, his father had announced his retirement. As good as that was for his parents, with it came a new set of responsibilities for Jarred, as well as his brothers.

"You and Brice have spent just as much time here," he said quietly, in his own defense.

"No, we haven't. As for Brice, this is the longest he's been around in a long time. We didn't even know that he and Nev were friends, let alone that he has a stake in her business. Face it, our brother cannot stay in any one place for an extended length of time. He has too much of a wanderlust spirit."

"Where is Brice, anyway?" Jarred asked. "I haven't seen his annoying self all week."

"He's been visiting the other branches."

"Why? Is there something going on that I don't know about?"

"No. According to Brice, he just wants to stay on top of things. I'm not aware of any issues, and if Brice is, he hasn't transmitted those concerns to me. Anyway, I'm out of here. I have a lot of paperwork to get through," Langston said, holding up the file in his hand.

"Keep me apprised of what's going on with that," Jarred said. "I would like to hear what this lady has to say about the information. I'm still thinking about just dumping Tempest."

"Your move. I'm with whatever you're comfortable with. You'll have to call a board meeting. Since dad is still the majority shareholder he has to be there, too."

"I know, Langston. Dad is the one who brought this mess to our door, anyway. I don't think he'll have a problem with it. I'll make him aware of everything before the meeting just in case. Speaking of our father, have you spoken to Mom?"

"I did. I called her on Mother's Day and I spoke with her on Saturday. She's still trying to figure out if Nev's pregnant," Langston said.

"I know. I haven't confirmed or denied the assumptions. I told Dad that Nevea could be pregnant and he ran with it. However, Nevea asked me not to say anything and I agreed, even though you all know, anyway. I spoke to Mom on Mother's Day, too. She wanted to know if I would be getting my young lady a card." Jarred snickered, and Langston burst out laughing.

"What did you say?"

"I told her if she wanted to be nosy she couldn't do it from Texas."

"Oh, I know she let you have it with that smart comment."

"Yep, she informed me that sons who love their mother would come to visit said mother," Jarred said drily.

"Ouch." Langston frowned.

"Who told them to retire all the way to Texas?"

"They aren't even old. They're only sixty-one and sixty," Langston said with a shrug.

"True. And most people retire to stop working. Dad retired to work harder."

"Now, that I still don't understand," Langston said with a shake of his head. He hefted the substantial file and made his way to the door. "I'll talk to you later. And Jarred?" he called over his shoulder.

Jarred lifted a questioning brow.

"Go get your woman. Remember there are two sides to her. You've been catering to the analytical part, but don't forget she owns Heavens and sings there. Speak to that side," Langston said, and walked out the door.

Jarred pondered that advice. His brother was dead right. Nevea had two distinct sides—the pragmatic, braniac techy and the creative, feminine, sensual side. Somehow Jarred needed to find a good balance between the two.

He sat there, thinking. Some time later—he had no idea how long—he knew just what he needed to do. Now the job was figuring out how to do it.

A slow smile crept across his lips. "I have the perfect solution," he said, and picked up his phone.

Chapter 21

Nevealise was sitting on the sunporch looking out on Cedric's backyard. Her mother was there fussing over her. It was the Memorial Day weekend and the only sound that broke the silence was the drone of lawnmowers and leaf blowers from the local yards.

She never could get used to the quiet in Cedric's neighborhood. No kids. No teenagers. Just the sound of car doors opening and closing in the morning and evenings when neighbors were going to work and then coming home. But nothing else. Not even a dog barking. Now that was creepy.

"You know, I'm glad Cedric's moving." Her mother's voice interrupted her musings.

Nevealise turned and smiled at her. "Why?"

"It's boring here," her mother huffed.

"You've only been here a few times, Mommy."

"You only have to go somewhere once to know if it's boring. I've been here more than a few times, dear. Still, this place as beautiful as it is, gives me the heebie-jeebies. Where are the children, dogs, a milk truck, something?" She looked so disgusted that Nevealise didn't have a choice but to laugh.

"A milk truck, Mommy? Really?"

"You know what I mean. This place reminds me of that movie—uh, you know, with those women... I think they were wives or something. Oh, why can't I remember the name of that movie?" She tsked.

"I don't know, Mommy. I don't watch much television. Sorry."

Her mother seemed to abandon her hunt for the movie title. Instead, she focused on her daughter, searching Nevealise's face. "How are you feeling, dear?"

"Better. I have the occasional bout of sickness. Nothing like it was before, though." Nevealise shivered.

"It gets better," her mother said, patting her on the knee. Just then the shrill sound of the doorbell rang through the house.

"You see? You see? That's not normal," her mother said, shaking her head in disgust, while at the same time getting up. "The loudest sound on the block should not be your doorbell. Strange."

Nevealise was laughing hard at her mother's antics. It was good to see Clara Tempest animated again, looking for fun, ready to enjoy life. Her mother actually seemed happy of late. Nevealise didn't know what was going on with her, but it was a welcome change. Not that her mother had ever been a bad person. *Unhappy* would be a better word. To see her joking around now was good.

Funny how life was. Instead of her mother seeming to be miserable, now the shoe was on the other foot. Not quite for the same reason, however. Whereas Josiah Tempest had made her mother feel like a maid, Jarred had never done that to Nevealise. In fact, he went out of his way to make sure she was taken care of and fed.

"Ooh, someone has an admirer," her mother declared. Nevealise turned her head to see her standing on the porch holding a long white box with a red ribbon with a neatly knotted bow wrapped around it.

"What's that?" she asked.

"I don't know, dear. Your name is on the box," she said, and set it on her lap.

"For me? Who would send me a present?" she whispered, untying the bow.

"Read the card first!" her mother cried.

"Mommy, you're more excited than I am," Nevealise said, picking up the tiny envelope. Just Because the card read and scrawled at the bottom was Yours, J.

"Well, who sent them?"

"They're from Jarred," she whispered, lifting the lid off the box. It was filled to the brim with long-stemmed red roses. Nevealise took one out, put it to her nose and inhaled its fragrance.

"Those are beautiful. And he sent a whole box of them, too." Clara Tempest looked closer. "There must be a few dozen roses in there."

"Yes, there are," she said softly.

"Mmm-hmm…that young man is serious. Why are we upset with him again?"

"Mommy, you know why," Nevealise murmured.

"Refresh my memory. You know I'm getting older, and if I'm going to be angry at this young man I have to remember why," her mother said, and sat down in the lounge chair next to hers. "Tell me again."

"Well…because—because…" Nevealise huffed.

"I thought so," her mother remarked slyly. She stood up again. "I'll make you some refreshments, and then I have to get going. I don't like to leave your father for too long."

"You don't have to fix anything, Mommy. I can order some takeout."

"I know. I'm just going to prepare a few finger foods. You can eat as much or as little as you want without feeling guilty."

"Okay. Thank you, Mommy."

"No problem." She stepped away, then turned back around. "I tell you, if I got a bunch of pretty flowers like that from a man, I sure would call and thank him. Yes, indeed. I may get some more then. They sure are pretty," her mother said, and started to leave the porch.

"I guess that's your way of telling me to call him," Nevealise called after her.

"No-o-o. You know I'm not one to meddle in my children's affairs. Not at all. But if it were me… Never mind." Her mother waved away what she was about to say, then stepped into the house.

But Nevealise got the message. Loud and clear.

She bit down on her bottom lip. Her mother was right. She did need to call Jarred to thank him for the beautiful roses. She'd missed his nightly calls. He had recently stopped phoning and started texting her instead. Text messages that contained funny and heart-shaped emojis.

She looked at the clock. It was only two in the afternoon. Even though it was a holiday weekend, she knew Jarred would be in the office. Should she call him there? Or maybe she should wait until he got home.

She wrestled with the decision for a full twenty minutes before picking up the phone and dialing.

"Nevea, what's wrong?" He sounded panicky.

"No…nothing's wrong. I called to thank you for the roses. They're beautiful."

"You got them already?" She could hear the smile in his voice.

"Yes, I did. My mother put them in a vase for me. We had to use two, there were so many."

"Beautiful flowers for a beautiful woman."

His response sent tingles down her spine. She'd often fall asleep at night thinking of Jarred's rich baritone voice, and of the song he'd sung to her at Heavens. Her mind often went back to that night—both his singing and his lovemaking. That decadent feeling of being sexed up against the door. And many nights she'd awaken aroused from dreams of the scene in her dressing room.

"Nevea, are you okay?" he was saying through the phone.

She chased away the thoughts and replied, "I'm fine. My bouts of sickness are subsiding. Certain smells and foods will still cause nausea, but most of the time, other than the tiredness I'm perfectly fine."

"Is the constant fatigue normal?"

"I don't know," she said wearily, placing her hand protectively over her baby bump. She already was in love with the little life that was growing inside her.

"What did the doctor say?"

Nevealise didn't respond right away. She didn't want to tell him that she hadn't seen an obstetrician yet.

She'd looked up countless doctors, but hadn't decided on one for fear of choosing the wrong doctor. One of her brother's doctor friends from the hospital had given her an initial checkup, with instructions to follow up with an ob-gyn. She'd gotten a clean bill of health, except for a low iron level. So every day she took her prenatal vitamins, as well as iron pills.

"Nevea, are you sure you're all right?"

"Yes, yes, I'm fine. Just a little spacey," she joked, and was rewarded with his husky chuckle. Oh, how she missed him. Everything about him.

"You never said what the doctor said about your exhaustion?" he prompted.

"That's because I haven't seen a doctor," she said hurriedly.

His silence scared her for a minute. He was sure to yell at her, she knew. She held her breath and waited for the chastisement.

Instead he asked softly, "Can I ask why not?"

Nevealise took the phone away from her ear and looked down at it, her brows furrowed. *What, no scorn? No telling me how I'm endangering the baby?* She waited. When he didn't say anything else she responded.

"I couldn't decide which one to use. I mean, there are so many choices. I didn't want to pick the wrong person," she muttered.

"Do you have a list?" he asked.

"Yes," she said hesitantly. Her hand instinctively caressed her belly.

"Do you want me to help you choose?"

Nevealise's heart filled with joy. Her hand motions against her stomach wavered. She hadn't realized until just this second that she wanted him to go with her. To help her with the decisions.

"If you wouldn't mind?"

"Nevea, of course I don't mind. What would make you think that I would? This is my baby, too," he said softly.

"I'm sorry. I just assumed."

"Can you email the list to me?"

"Yes."

"When will you send it?"

"Just as soon as I get off of the phone with you."

"You said your mother helped you with the flowers?"

"Yes, she comes by a few times a week to keep me company. The house is so quiet. Cedric's hardly ever here," she sighed.

"Are you bored?"

"Out of my mind," she said quickly, and he started laughing.

"If you'd like I can stop by tomorrow and we can go for a drive or something. Maybe even hang out at my house in the Hamptons for a day or two."

"I'd like that."

"You would?" he asked, as if he hadn't heard her.

"Yes. I'd like that a lot. I'm going stir-crazy in this place."

"That's because you're used to being busy."

"That is true. I know you're working. I'll let you get back to it. I just wanted to thank you for the flowers. They were so lovely I couldn't wait until you got home from work."

"Don't worry about it. You don't need to thank me for sending you flowers. You deserve that and much more. Call me anytime you feel like it. It's not a problem. I'm available to you anytime."

"I will. Thanks again, Jarred. I'll see you tomorrow."

"See you tomorrow, Nevea."

Her heart swelled at the use of the name he'd gifted her with at Heavens. When she hung up she was smiling from ear to ear.

Josiah Tempest sat out in the garden waiting for his wife to come home. Today, as always, he felt tired, sad and lonely. Josiah had certainly made a mess out of things with his children and his wife. While Clara had forgiven him, he doubted his children ever would. Especially his only daughter. She hated him so much.

If Josiah was honest with himself, he should have never married the beautiful and brilliant Clara McMorris. But he'd taken one look at her and had been smitten with the woman ten years his junior. Besides, if he hadn't wed her, then he wouldn't have the three beautiful children that Clara had borne him. Intelligent children.

From the very beginning, he'd been too blinded by jealousy to be the man he should have been. Josiah had seen the way his colleagues and other men looked at Clara. Like they wanted her. As if they wondered why she was with him, instead of one of them. And for good reason, he realized too late. She was a beautiful woman, one he had clearly taken advantage of. Most of the antics he pulled with his wife were to keep her with him. He'd been so afraid of losing her to someone else that he did the unthinkable: He mistreated her. It was a wonder Clara had stayed with him. Any other woman would have left long ago. Especially after the children had gone off to college.

"Oh, here you are."

Josiah turned to smile when he heard his wife's voice. At sixty-five she was still as beautiful and as regal as ever.

"How was your visit with Nevealise?" Josiah had never called her by the nickname that everyone else used, preferring to stick with her given name rather than Nev.

"It was fine. I think our daughter is starting to come around. You should've seen her face when Jarred sent her a few dozen long-stemmed roses," Clara said, beaming as she did so.

Josiah smiled again. "He did that?"

"Yes, he did. So how are you feeling today?"

"I'm okay, Clara. You can stop fussing over me." He grinned. "I'm more interested in Nevealise. How's she feeling?" he asked anxiously.

"She's much better. Now what do you feel like having for supper?"

"How do you fancy going out?"

Josiah was deeply saddened by the shocked expression on her face. He'd truly done his family a disservice.

"You're up to going out?" she questioned.

"Clara, I have a bad heart and a case of chronic obstructive pulmonary disease 'COPD.' I'm not dead. I don't think a little night out is going to kill me," he retorted.

"If you're sure…"

"Positive." He rose from his chair to go inside. "By the time I get dressed it should be time for dinner."

"Oh, pooh. You're not that slow and you know it. I'll wash up, too, and meet you in the drawing room," she said as she stepped into the house.

"Clara?" he called.

She turned to him. "Yes, Jo?"

"I love you. I always have," he whispered. Her eyes watered, and that brought tears to his own eyes.

"I know, but thank you for saying it," she murmured.

Chapter 22

Jarred watched as Nevea lay on a lounge chair in front of his in-ground pool. He'd picked her up from Cedric's yesterday and they'd spent most of the day looking for an obstetrician. After finally calling and finding one that they both seemed to like, they'd made an appointment. Since it was the Memorial Day weekend they couldn't have an appointment until the following week. To say he was excited was an understatement.

He stared at her. She was beautiful, lying there in the sun in a lovely one-piece bathing suit with a sarong cover-up and dark sunglasses. Her baby bump was visible, but not by much. She looked content.

Jarred couldn't hide his surprise when she'd agreed to stay with him in the Hamptons. This was what he'd been waiting for since their misunderstanding. A chance to be alone with her, to hold her in his arms and tell her how much he loved and adored her.

"Are you hungry?" he asked, settling in a lounger next to her.

"Not at all. I'm just relaxing. Feels good out here," she sighed.

"How's Junior holding up?"

Nivea lifted her shades and turned to him. The surprised look on her face almost sent him into a fit of laughter. "What do you mean, Junior? You know it could be a girl," she said with a sniff.

"Could be. But I'm thinking it's a boy," he stated.

"We'll find out soon enough," she said, her palm automatically going to her abdomen.

Jarred stared at her hand. He had yet to feel the growth of their baby in her belly. Without giving it a second thought, he reached out and covered Nevea's hand with his. "I don't care what the baby is as long as he or she is healthy."

"Do you know what?" she whispered.

"What?" He raised a brow.

"I am scared spitless. I mean, I can't even remember to feed myself. How am I going to take care of a baby?"

"Nevea, sweetheart, don't worry about it. It'll come naturally to you. And you're already taking better care of yourself. Don't forget I'm here, and I'm not going anywhere. I'm in your life and my baby's, to stay. So get used to it," he said matter-of-factly. "Besides you and I, our parents are there, too. You know they're going to spoil the little one to pieces. Right after my mother brains me," Jarred said with a snort.

Nev's look of shock made him chuckle. "Why would she do that? Your mother is one of the nicest people I know."

"True. She is. But when she finds out I got you pregnant, she's going to have my head on a platter."

"Oh, no! Jarred, you didn't tell them, did you?" she asked, panicked.

"Nevea, I don't have to tell them. They'll find out soon enough. You forget our parents are friends," he reminded her.

"Honestly, I never thought about it. Ugh, I am such a dunce," she moaned.

"No, you're not. You've had a lot on your mind of late. And let's not forget the morning sickness."

"More like morning, noon and night sickness. I am so glad that's almost over with. Now I just wish this lethargy would go away," she groaned.

"It will. The iron pills that Cedric's doctor friend prescribed aren't working?" Jarred asked.

"Not really. Cedric's going to fax the new doctor the initial blood workup."

"Good. You're drinking enough water to keep from being dehydrated, right?"

"Yes, I believe so. I've cut out all caffeine after my sickness subsided. My appetite is random still. I'm thinking that's from not wanting to eat for fear of vomiting. I hate that. Ugh." She cringed.

"What do you fancy having for lunch?"

"Whatever you're having." She looked around the pool area. "This place is so beautiful, Jarred. Will your family be here for the weekend?"

He shrugged. "I don't know. I didn't want to presume that you wanted my family around."

She speared him with a look, even though he couldn't exactly see her eyes behind her sunglasses. "Jarred, why wouldn't I want your family around? I love your brothers. And by the way, where's Kat? I haven't heard any of you speak of her."

"I haven't a clue where Kat is at the moment. She's in design school and she also travels a lot. Besides, the only people she checks in with are the parents. She says that Langston, Brice and I are just a little too overbearing. Her words, not mine," he explained.

"I could just imagine. I have two brothers, so I know. Cedric's pretty good. Elijah, however, is another story. For some reason he thinks he's my father rather than my brother. I miss him, but goodness, he's a pain in the behind," she said lovingly.

"Considering what you went through with your father, can you blame him?"

"I guess not." Her scowl deepened.

"Have you spoken to him?"

"Who?"

"Your dad," Jarred said quietly.

"No, not yet. He asks how I'm doing through my mother," she said quietly.

"So he knows about the baby?" Jarred questioned.

"Yes. He knows."

"You may not want to hear this, but I think he did what he did, as far as the company is concerned, to protect you. There was some real shady stuff going on there."

"I kind of sense that from all the cloak-and-dagger stuff. I can't figure out why your dad would buy the company knowing that it was falling apart."

"I guess he was trying to help a friend out," Jarred said.

"I suppose." She was quiet a moment before she spoke again. "Will my father go to jail?"

"I don't believe he will, but I don't know. For all his other faults, Nevea, Josiah Tempest is a brilliant businessman. There's still a long way to go, but I believe he's out of it. Keeping *us* out of this mess is the challenge now." Jarred and his brothers and Emerson were still going through the records. Among the many other issues they had to deal with, corporate espionage was a serious charge.

His assurances about her father must have worked on her, because Nevea didn't pursue the subject. Instead, she spoke about her mother. "She seems much cheerier now. I don't know what's going on, but she jokes around and smiles a great deal. She's happy."

"Maybe she and your dad have worked out their differences," Jarred said.

"Hmm, I don't know. I never ask. My mother is happy and that's all that concerns me," Nevealise said.

Jarred suddenly realized that his hand was still covering her belly. He looked down at it. It felt right. This close to her, he figured it was finally time to make right the wrong he'd done to her. Removing his hand, he swung his feet down and turned in his seat to face her.

"Come here, Nevea," he said quietly, taking her by the hand, helping her up and pulling her onto his lap. She looked nervous.

"There's nothing to fear, Nevea. Let me say this, and please don't interrupt me. Just let me say what I have to say. Can you do that?" he asked. Once he got her nod of approval, he proceeded. "I realize that I jumped to the wrong conclusions that night, and I sincerely regret that. You hadn't given me any cause to doubt your faithfulness to our relationship. I was putting old hurts onto you and it wasn't fair. All I'm asking now is that you give us a chance. I love you with all of my heart. It's taken me a little while to come to terms with it. However, I have. Now I'm asking that you give me, you and our baby a chance to be a family. A real family," he said softly.

"Jarred, what are you saying?" she whispered.

"I'm saying that I want you to become my wife, Nevea."

"For the sake of the baby?" she asked.

"Oh, I guess you missed the part where I said that I love you. I love you, sweetheart," he repeated, this time slowly, "and I suspect that I always will." He ran a finger down the side of her face. Nevea closed her eyes and buried her cheek in his hand.

"Our lives are so different, Jarred," she murmured.

"And?" he questioned.

"I don't know if it will work out. Look at my parents…"

"No, let's not look at your parents." He cut in with a shake of his head. "Answer me this. Do you love me, Nevea?" He held his breath and waited for her response. Each second she was quiet was like a stab in his heart. Jarred needed to hear the words. If she couldn't say them now, he'd love her so much she would have no other choice but to marry him. And he hoped someday he could earn her trust enough for her to love him in return.

"Jarred, do you seriously think that I would have given my body to you if I didn't love you? I've crushed on you since I was, like, sixteen."

"Sixteen! Really? I thought it was eighteen, according to—never mind. You were saying?" He smiled, knowing she was about to say what he wanted to hear. He wanted the words to actually come from her lips.

"As I was saying—" she stressed the words and rolled her eyes "—of course I love you. I wouldn't put so much energy into anything that I didn't think…"

Jarred didn't hear another thing she said. All he heard was that she loved him. His insides were doing flip-flops.

"Nevea, sweetheart, we are not a science project to be dissected. You loving me is all I need to hear." He pulled her head down and met her tongue with his. It had been too long since they'd kissed, since he'd made love to her. He was about to change that. "Let's go inside. I don't want to give any nosy neighbor a peek at my woman."

They walked side by side into the house, where Jarred led her to the master suite.

He came to a stop in front of the bed, looked down into her hazel eyes and whispered, "I love you, Nevea."

"I love you, too," Nevealise said, wrapping her arms around him.

Jarred stepped back and lifted her chin up so that her lips met his. He parted her mouth with his tongue and kissed her with the hunger of a starving man.

He grabbed her by her hips and lifted her up into his erection, rubbing against her. Jarred walked her backward until her knees hit the bed, and then pushed her down gently. He followed, lying half on top of her, brought his mouth back down to hers and kissed her passionately.

His hand roamed freely across her sensitive breast.

"Ah!" She cried out and bucked against him.

"Do they hurt?" he asked breathlessly.

"Yes. A good pain, though," she moaned. Jarred continued to tweak her breast between his thumb and forefinger. She writhed against him.

Slipping his fingers under the sarong, he shed it with ease, then went to work on the straps of her swimsuit, pulling them down until her breasts lay bare for him to see. They were fuller, no doubt from the pregnancy. Not being able to wait any longer, he leaned over and brought one hardened nipple into his mouth and suckled. Nevea went wild beneath him. Jarred continued his assault on her breasts, moving from one to the other. When his mouth finally left them, she cried out. "No!"

"Easy, baby," he said, seeking her lips. Her mouth opened under his. That was all the encouragement Jarred needed. He took over the kiss, his tongue latching on to hers. Their tongues danced in harmony.

Nevealise hadn't realized how horny she was until Jarred started making love to her. She'd missed him oh so much, and apparently so did her body.

She marveled at the feel of his tongue inside her mouth. Jarred knew how to please her in every way. She felt her bathing suit being dragged down her body, slowly, sensually. Her hips rose slightly to allow him the room to remove the suit. And then she was naked before him.

Jarred's lips left hers to place little kisses all over her, across her neck and down between her breasts.

"Oh, Jarred, that feels so good," she purred.

"Baby, you haven't felt anything yet," Jarred murmured as his tongue slid across her breast. Nevealise gasped with pleasure. Throwing her head back against the pillow, she crooned out her desire.

Under his tender touches, Nevealise was about to come unglued. Jarred manipulated her body like a well-played instrument. He knew exactly what chords to press, pluck and pull. In minutes she was already at the crest of an orgasm, though Jarred hadn't gotten started yet.

Her ragged cries for him to fill her urged him on. She began to writhe against him in hopes that he would give her what she wanted: him inside her. Filling her to the brim. Nevealise's already sexually charged body began to heat up even more until she was sure one more lave of her breast would send her over the edge.

"Jarred," she murmured. "I don't think I can hold on for much longer."

Jarred released her nipple, got up from the bed and quickly shucked his clothes. He then returned to her. "Wait no longer, beautiful," he whispered breathlessly. In one smooth motion he parted her legs with his and slid inside her.

"Oh wow! Oh jeez!" Nevealise chanted, as sensation after sensation flooded through her. She began to move her body in tune with his. As quickly as his thrusts started, Nevealise found herself straddling him.

"You said you learned some new moves, Nevea," he drawled. "Show me what you're working with, baby. Take your pleasure."

Nevealise looked into his beautiful eyes surrounded by dark lashes. They were smoky with passion. She gazed down at him, a bit confused. However, it felt as if he were touching her womb, and it felt oh so good.

"You want me to…"

"Ride it like you stole it, baby. Ride it like you stole

it," he breathed out, half teasing. "This way you're in control. Have your way with me."

And have her way she did.

"Damn, Nevea! Baby, you're trying to kill me," he said coarsely.

Nevealise was close. So close she could feel her toes tingling. Sweat beaded on her skin; sensations overwhelmed her senses. Feeling as if she were going to pass out from pleasure, she dug her nails into Jarred's shoulders, threw her head back and cried in release. Jarred grabbed her by the hips, pushed up into her once more and then came, emptying himself inside her.

So spent she could hardly catch her breath, Nevealise fell on top on him. With her head on his muscled chest, she could hear each beat of his heart.

"Sweetheart, are you all right?" he asked anxiously.

"Better than all right. Wow!" she cried. "Wow!"

A chuckle rumbled in his chest. "It was pretty amazing. Babe, I said ride me, not kill me," he teased. "What the hell, you had horse riding lessons or something?"

Nevealise swatted him on the chest. Her face reddened. He loved to make her blush by saying the most outrageous things.

"You know you still didn't answer my question," he said quietly, his fingers cruising up and down her spine.

"What question was that?" she asked.

"Will you marry me?"

"Yes," she said without hesitation.

"Yes!" he screamed, and then bucked, almost knocking her off him. "Oh, baby, I'm sorry," he said, wrapping his arms more tightly around her. "First thing in the morning we are going for a ring."

"We can wait until next week, Jarred," she said.

"Oh no, we can't. And we can get married before the baby comes, most definitely. Do you want a large or small wedding?" he asked.

"Small. Just family and a few friends," she said.

"Good. Let's tell the families!" he cried excitedly.

"Tomorrow. I'm sleepy now." To emphasize her words, she yawned.

"Sure. Rest, baby," he said, then he turned with Nevea in his arms and waited until she fell asleep. Then he slid from under her, grabbed a pair of pajama bottoms and slipped out of the room.

Jarred dialed Brice first.

"Nevea and I are getting married," he blurted out, barely waiting for his brother to answer the phone.

"Married?" Brice sounded confused.

"Yes, married. We love one another and we're having a baby together. We're going to make it legal."

"Better you than me. Hey, congratulations, man! Now maybe you'll stop terrorizing the employees."

"Thanks, man. Let me call Langston," Jarred said.

"You better call the folks first."

"Nope. Mom will keep me on the phone the entire night. You call her. Tell her I'll call her tomorrow. I left Nevea in bed. I want to get back before she wakes up."

"Oh. It will be your head she bashes," Brice kidded. "Congrats again. Give Nev my best."

"Will do. Thanks, man, for everything," Jarred said, knowing Brice would hear the sincerity in his voice.

"No problem. What are brothers for?" he said nonchalantly.

Jarred disconnected the call and dialed Langston. He got his brother's voice mail and told him the news.

"Talk to you soon, Langston. Don't call me until tomorrow 'cause I'm heading back where I belong—in bed."

When he finally went back to join Nevea, he pulled her naked body into his arms. She stirred, murmured something and then relaxed against him.

Yeah, he was exactly where he belonged.

Epilogue

Nevealise and Jarred were married in the backyard of Jarred's Southampton home two weeks after their announcement. Nevea wanted to get married before she started to show too much. The design of her dress covered her baby bump very well. Part of Jarred's vow was to love her forever, and she believed him.

Nevealise had somewhat made peace with her father, at her mother's instance. She really couldn't hold too much of a grudge, since her mom was still with him, and they both seemed to be happy. Nevealise had even let her father walk her down the aisle. Josiah had cried probably more than she had. She'd known her father was sick, but up until a week before the wedding, when she'd gone to her parents' home with Jarred to ask her father to escort her down the aisle, she hadn't fully comprehended just how sick her father was. He was thin and drawn. Not the robust, handsome man of long ago.

Nevealise smiled at the remembrance of her wedding. What was supposed to have been a private ceremony had included over a hundred people.

Jarred had laughed and joked about it, saying, "Baby, just think of what would have happened had we given them more time." He was right, of course. Nevealise didn't know how their mothers had pulled it off, but it was a beautiful ceremony. She was happy. Ecstatically so.

Nevealise now sat in a honeymoon suite in the Poconos, not wanting to go far because of her condition. The doctor had said that she was severely anemic, and had arranged for a hematologist to monitor her. Nevealise had been afraid beyond belief. Jarred, her mother and his mother had all been wonderful, consoling her and reminding her not to borrow trouble where there was none. She'd taken their advice after the scan had showed that the baby was fine, and that they were having a girl. Nevealise would need to be monitored closely, and have scans done more frequently than usual until they got her anemia under control. Both her brothers had donated blood just in case she would need a transfusion after delivery.

"You okay, Nevea?" she heard her husband ask. *Husband.* The word was music to her ears. Never would she have imagined getting married, but here she was, not only married, but expecting a baby.

"I'm more than okay, husband of mine." She smiled.

"You were so engrossed in your thoughts that I wondered," he said.

"I'm not worked up about my anemia anymore,

Jarred. However, I do need my husband to make love to me. I mean, that is why we have this pretty honeymoon suite, isn't it?" she sassed.

"I see someone's got a healthy appetite for more than just food." Jarred chuckled.

"Are you complaining?" she purred, and stretched out on the bed.

"Not in this lifetime," he declared. Jarred leaned forward, removed Nevea's skimpy gown, and then his boxers. Using his knees, he parted her legs, aligned his erection with her opening and gently pushed inside.

"Yes-s-s," Nevealise breathed.

"Ah, baby, you feel so good. I don't know how long I'm going to last," Jarred groaned, increasing his tempo. Taking her lips in a scorching kiss, he lifted her hips, sinking deeper into her. He began to trail kisses across her face, her neck and her shoulder.

Jarred felt Nevealise clenching around him and prayed he could hold on for her release. As if she was in his head, she bucked against him and cried out. Jarred followed her over the edge, calling her name as he did so.

"I love you so much, Nevea," he growled. Jarred waiting for their breathing to calm before speaking again. "You are my everything, sweetheart. Words cannot express how much I love you."

"Love me forever," she whispered. "Just love me forever."

"No doubt about it, baby. Through thick and thin, we are in this forever."

"I want to thank you, Bill, for giving me my daughter back," Josiah Tempest said to his longtime friend, as he gripped the phone tightly in his hand. Josiah's gaze traveled the expanse of the room. Golden light trickled through the oversized windows and painted soft rectangles against the wooden floors. This brought a smile to his face. He loved the newly renovated bedroom. Clara had done a wonderful job in redecorating it. The room was warm and inviting. The scent from the floral arrangement on the table across the room was divine. Even if lungs couldn't absorb them to their full capacity. The look and smell of the weekly blooms always brought a smile to his face.

"For what?"

Josiah sighed weakly. "I've been a first-rate fool for many years," he said, with his breath wheezing through his lungs.

"Well, now, I really can't argue with that." William Manning chuckled. "We all make mistakes, Josiah. Yours was a big one. However, friends don't abandon friends in times of trouble."

"I never thought I'd have my family back," Josiah whispered, as a lone tear rolled down his face.

"Well, you had a chance to make it right and you have. Just move forward from here and let the past go. Besides, soon we'll have this grandbaby we need to spoil. I have to say, when you came to me with this harebrained scheme of yours, I didn't have a clue that it would lead to our children getting married." William shook his head and smiled. "Dee's still on cloud nine."

"So is Clara. She's already shopping for that baby, and Nevealise's not due until winter." Josiah started laughing, then had to wait to speak until he stopped coughing.

"You okay, Josiah?" William asked. Josiah could

hear the concern in his voice and was forever grateful for his friend. "Is Clara there with you?"

"What? Your hearing getting bad in your old age, Bill?" Josiah teased. "Clara's out."

"Man, I'm not old. Just ask Dee," William Manning said. "*You're* old."

Josiah laughed. "You think they'll ever figure out they were swindled to get Nevealise there?"

"Nah, this was actually good for them. And you did have a lot going on in that company, Josiah. You know you could have gone to jail from that mess. However, you handled it well. Nah, I'll give my boys a little more time before I suggest they dump Tempest. Who knows, maybe I'll get some more grandbabies out of this mess."

"You just may. So I did a good deed, didn't I?" Josiah asked.

"I would say so, my friend. I would say so."

"Good. I needed to hear that." Josiah wheezed and coughed again.

"Josiah, are you sure you're okay? You don't sound so good, man."

"I am now, Bill. I am now. I guess Clara is back. I hear shopping bags," Josiah joshed.

"I can only imagine. I don't know how Dee is going to get all these packages from Texas to New York," William grunted, and sent Josiah into another fit of wheezing.

"She'll find a way, my friend." Josiah breathed deeply in and out. "Again, thanks for everything. Kiss my grandbaby for me," he said, and took his last breath.

"What do you mean?" When William heard no response, he called, "Josiah? Josiah, are you still there? Josiah. Josiah!" he yelled into the phone.

Instead of his longtime friend's voice, a hysterical Clara was heard on the line. "He's gone, Bill."

"Oh damn," William Manning whispered, and then mourned his friend.

Jarred awoke to the loud chirping of his cell phone. Looking at the clock on the night table next to the bed, he furrowed his brow. It wasn't late, but the rushed planning of the wedding and all the doctor visits had worn out both him and Nevea. Not to mention their incessant lovemaking. He'd made love to her, albeit gently, more times than he thought was healthy, but his wife's hormones were kicking into overdrive and their doctor had assured them sex wouldn't harm her or the baby.

Jarred grabbed his cell phone and looked at the caller ID. Why was his father calling? Jarred got a sinking feeling in the pit of his stomach. His dad would never disturb his honeymoon unless it was something serious. Quietly leaving the bed, Jarred made his way out of the bedroom and into the living room of their honeymoon suite.

"Dad," he said gruffly.

"Hey, son. I'm sorry to interrupt your time alone with Nevealise, but I'm afraid I have some bad news."

Jarred swallowed hard. He prayed nothing was wrong with his mom. "What is it, Dad?"

"I'm afraid Josiah passed earlier today. We contemplated waiting till you got home, but I didn't feel right about not telling you. If you decide to wait to tell

Nevealise, that's fine. Nothing will be done until you all get back, anyway."

Jarred couldn't deny his concern. He worried that this news would be something else stressful his pregnant wife would have to deal with.

"Ah, man. Shit! Yeah, I'll figure out a way to tell her. She'll want to be there for her mom, anyway."

"I thought so, too. Clara was adamant about not contacting her, but I didn't feel it was right."

"No, you're correct. I'm sorry for your loss, Dad. I know you and Mr. Tempest were good pals," he said.

"He had his faults, Jarred, but he was still my friend." Jarred could hear his father's voice break.

"It'll be okay, Dad. We'll be back in the morning. No sense in waking Nevea now," Jarred whispered. "When are you flying in?"

"Your mother and I are flying out sometime tomorrow, I guess. I'll see you when I get there."

"Talk to you soon, Dad," Jarred said, and then disconnected. Now he had to figure out how to break the news to his wife. She'd just patched things up with her father, and now he was gone.

Josiah Tempest was laid to rest less than a week later. He was survived by his wife of many years and his three adult children.

Nevealise and Jarred remained at the graveside long after the other mourners had gone to their cars.

"Are you okay, sweetheart?" Jarred asked his wife.

"I'm okay. At least we got to settle our differences before he passed. I don't think I could have lived with myself otherwise," she said, her voice cracking.

"It's okay, love. Let it all out," he said, grabbing her in his arms and letting her cry.

Afterward, they went back to the house for a small repast. When the last guest left, her brothers assured them they were going to stay with their mother to get things settled, so Jarred took Nevea home.

Now he sat up in bed, watching the soft rise and fall of her chest. She'd finally gone off to sleep. He ran a tired hand over his face, and then pulled Nevea into his arms, placing his hand on her belly. He was home.

Jarred had found a peace within himself that he never knew existed. He knew within his heart of hearts that Nevea was the cause of his inner peace. She was more than he could have asked for in a wife and the mother of his unborn child. He would love both of them forever, till death did them part.

Jarred smiled, snuggled closer to his wife and quickly joined her in sleep.

* * * * *

SPECIAL EXCERPT FROM

*Faith Alexander's guardian angel has a body built for
sin. Ever since she woke up in the hospital after a car
crash, her rescuer, Brandon Gray, has been by her side—
chivalrous, caring and oh-so-fine. All Brandon's focus is
on his long-coveted role as CEO—until he stops to help
a mysterious beauty. With chemistry this irresistible, he's
ready to share a future with Faith, but he feels beyond
betrayed to discover what she's been hiding. If desire
and trust can overcome pride, he'll realize he's found the
perfect partner in the boardroom and the bedroom...*

*Read on for a sneak peek at
GIVING MY ALL TO YOU, the next exciting
installment in author Sheryl Lister's*
THE GRAYS OF LOS ANGELES *series!*

She frowned. *Who in the world...?* As if sensing her scrutiny,
he opened his eyes and pushed up from the chair. Faith blinked.
He was even taller than she originally thought, well-built and
easily the most handsome man she'd seen in a long time.

"Hey," he said softly.

"I thought I dreamed you."

His deep chuckle filled the room. "No. I'm very real."

Faith tried to clear the cobwebs from her mind. "You helped
me when I crashed." She thought for a moment. "Brandon?"

He nodded. "How are you feeling?"

"Everything hurts. Even breathing hurts." She closed her
eyes briefly. "Um...what time is it?" she murmured.

Brandon checked his watch. "A little after eleven."

KPEXP0417

"You've been here all this time?"

"For the most part. I brought your stuff and I didn't want to leave it with anyone without your permission." He placed them on the tray.

"Thank you."

"Do you want me to call your husband or family?"

Faith wanted to roll her eyes at the husband reference, but just the thought made her ache, so she settled for saying "I'm not married."

"What about family—Mom, Dad?"

The last person she wanted to talk to was her mother. "My parents don't live here," she added softly. She had been on her way to her father's house, but chickened out before arriving and had turned around to go back to the hotel when she'd had the accident.

A frown creased his brow. "You don't have anyone here?"

"No. I live in Oregon. I just got here yesterday."

"Hell of a welcome."

"Tell me about it," she muttered.

"Well, now that I know you're okay, I'm going to leave. I'll stop by to see you tomorrow to make sure you don't need anything." Brandon covered her uninjured hand with his large one and gave it a gentle squeeze.

Despite every inch of her body aching, the warmth of his touch sent an entirely different sensation flowing through her. The intense way he was staring at her made her think he had felt something, as well.

"I…um…" Brandon eased his hand from hers. "Get some rest." However, he didn't move, his interest clear as glass. After another moment he walked to the door, but turned back once more. "Good night."

"Good night." Faith watched as he slipped out the door, her heart still racing. Her life seemed to be a mess right now, but knowing she would see Brandon again made her smile.

Don't miss GIVING MY ALL TO YOU
by Sheryl Lister, available May 2017
wherever Harlequin® Kimani Romance™
books and ebooks are sold.

Copyright © 2017 by Sheryl Lister

KPEXP0417

Get 2 Free Books,
Plus 2 Free Gifts—
just for trying the Reader Service!

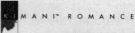 KIMANI™ ROMANCE

YES! Please send me 2 FREE Harlequin® Kimani™ Romance novels and my 2 FREE gifts (gifts are worth about $10 retail). After receiving them, if I don't wish to receive any more books, I can return the shipping statement marked "cancel." If I don't cancel, I will receive 4 brand-new novels every month and be billed just $5.69 per book in the U.S. or $6.24 per book in Canada. That's a savings of at least 12% off the cover price. It's quite a bargain! Shipping and handling is just 50¢ per book in the U.S. and 75¢ per book in Canada.* I understand that accepting the 2 free books and gifts places me under no obligation to buy anything. I can always return a shipment and cancel at any time. Even if I never buy another book, the 2 free books and gifts are mine to keep forever.

168/368 XDN GLQK

Name	(PLEASE PRINT)	

Address		Apt. #

City	State/Prov.	Zip/Postal Code

Signature (if under 18, a parent or guardian must sign)

Mail to the **Reader Service:**
IN U.S.A.: P.O. Box 1867, Buffalo, NY 14240-1867
IN CANADA: P.O. Box 611, Fort Erie, Ontario L2A 9Z9

Want to try two free books from another line?
Call 1-800-873-8635 or visit www.ReaderService.com.

*Terms and prices subject to change without notice. Prices do not include applicable taxes. Sales tax applicable in NY. Canadian residents will be charged applicable taxes. Offer not valid in Quebec. This offer is limited to one order per household. Books received may not be as shown. Not valid for current subscribers to Harlequin® Kimani™ Romance books. All orders subject to credit approval. Credit or debit balances in a customer's account(s) may be offset by any other outstanding balance owed by or to the customer. Please allow 4 to 6 weeks for delivery. Offer available while quantities last.

Your Privacy—The Reader Service is committed to protecting your privacy. Our Privacy Policy is available online at www.ReaderService.com or upon request from the Reader Service.

We make a portion of our mailing list available to reputable third parties that offer products we believe may interest you. If you prefer that we not exchange your name with third parties, or if you wish to clarify or modify your communication preferences, please visit us at www.ReaderService.com/consumerschoice or write to us at Reader Service Preference Service, P.O. Box 9062, Buffalo, NY 14240-9062. Include your complete name and address.

KROM17R

There's no mistaking the real thing

Bridget Anderson

The Only One for

Me

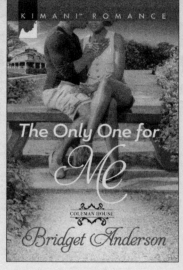

KIMANI™ ROMANCE

The Only One for

Me

COLEMAN HOUSE

Bridget Anderson

Running the shop at her family's B and B offers Corra Coleman a fresh start after her unhappy marriage—and a tantalizing temptation in the form of millionaire Christopher Williams. With Corra's ex trying to win her back, can Chris show her how love is supposed to be?

COLEMAN HOUSE

Available April 2017!

"Humor, excitement, great secondary characters, a mystery worked throughout the story and a great villain all make Anderson's latest an especially strong book." —*RT Book Reviews* on *HOTEL PARADISE*

HARLEQUIN®
™ www.Harlequin.com

KPBA495

Every wish will be fulfilled

Sherelle Green

Nights of Fantasy

From the moment real estate mogul Jaleen Walker meets Danni Allison, their physical connection is electric, but she's holding something back. Revealing her background could cost her the beautiful life she's built. Will five nights together be enough for them to stop keeping secrets…and lose their hearts to each other?

BARE SOPHISTICATION

Available April 2017!

"The love scenes are steamy and passionate, and the storyline is fast-paced and well-rounded."
—*RT Book Reviews* on *IF ONLY FOR TONIGHT*

HARLEQUIN®
www.Harlequin.com

KPSG494

Can he open her heart to more than a fleeting passion?

DEBORAH FLETCHER MELLO

When Kamaya Boudreaux's secret venture—an exclusive male-strip-club franchise—is threatened to be exposed, she needs to do damage control. But she doesn't know her lover, Wesley Walters, was formally the top performer at the high-end New Orleans nightclub. Wes must come clean—or lose the guarded beauty…

THE BOUDREAUX FAMILY

●●●

Available April 2017!

"Drama, hot sex, attention to detail and a thrilling storyline filled with twists and turns make this book a hard one to put down. A must read."
—*RT Book Reviews* on *HEARTS AFIRE*

HARLEQUIN®
www.Harlequin.com

KPDFM493